MAYBE I SHOULD DRIVE

OR BOYS ARE CRAZY BUT GIRLS AREN'T ALWAYS CLUELESS

HEATHER KELLY

*For all those sisters
who secretly think the sun rises and sets on
their brothers.*

CONTENTS

CHAPTER 1

NEVER PUSH THE BIG PINK BUTTON

Sometimes boys are crazy. Okay, most times. Although, if you asked my brother, he'd tell you that girls are, very often, clueless.

You can't ask Tim though, because he's screaming his lungs out while running in circles behind me. Well, running in oblongs, anyway.

One second ago, I was hanging out of my second-floor bedroom window clutching (and stretching out) the elastic on the waist of Tim's shorts to keep him from falling to his death, and Tim was yelling some nonsense like, "Kelly, just let me go, I'll tuck and roll!" because he secretly thinks he's a movie stuntman.

Then we both fell, a half-second ago, but we didn't hit the ground; we slurped into some invisible spaceship.

How can I tell? I'm staring at the control panel right now. A silvery sloped counter top with blinking lights and dials, right below a huge picture window.

My little brother has made me sit through enough sci-fi movies this year for me to identify a spaceship's innards at first glance.

I park myself into the white thing in front of me that looks remarkably like an Earth chair.

Ignoring how the chair pinches my normal-sized (thank you very much) butt, I float my fingers above all the noodle-y-looking buttons and nobs, careful not to touch a thing.

Touching is my brother's area of expertise. It's why we're always in these stupid messes.

A quarter of a second ago, my best friend Sarah and her brother Casey fell through the same invisible hole we did.

You know when your mom asks, "If your friends jumped off a cliff, would you jump too?" Not that cliff-jumping is my litmus test for loyalty. But these friends did jump out the window after us.

Best. Friends. Ever.

I look above where we slid into this ship and don't see any hole there, just the bluish-silvery arc of a ceiling above us.

I don't know how this spaceship works—maybe the top opens up like a soft-top convertible?

All I know is it's invisible from outside, but inside it's a sea of pastels with a huge shimmering window showing a great big closeup of the tree in my backyard.

Now there are *two* boys running oblongs behind me and one best friend spinning in slow circles with her mouth hanging open.

Mouth-hanging-open is traditionally an unflattering look—it certainly is on me—but somehow Sarah does it like she does everything else—with style.

I should feel upset that Sarah and her little brother are now in this stupid ship too, since all my internal *Danger! Warning! Danger!* alarms are buzzing like crazy.

I'd have to be a bad friend to wish any danger on my best friend, but I'm going to be honest, I'm a little relieved.

If you're going to get trapped in a weird space ship with anyone, you'd want it to be Sarah.

A sizzling sound zips my attention back to the spaceship's console. Not like bacon sizzling on the stove, more like recently-poured soda sizzling next to your ear.

I fondly think of my Coke at breakfast and wish I was back at our kitchen table, which really isn't that far away.

If we can fall into this ship, maybe we can just fall back out? I reach toward the tree branch looming in front of me, expecting my hand to push right through the shimmering window between me and normalcy.

Instead, I touch a soft, slightly warm, pliable plastic-like substance that hardens when I push on it.

I push harder on the not-glass window.

I want to be on the other side of it. I want to climb out of this ship and into the tree beyond.

I want to enjoy my planned Saturday of ignoring my brother and hanging out with Sarah. I want to finish my breakfast grilled cheese and sip from a fresh can of Coke.

The sizzling sound grows insistent.

I angrily push the not-glass as hard as I can, which starts my chair slowly spinning. Only increasing the pinching-butt sensation.

My slow-motion spin enables a fantastic view of the craziness behind me. The cavernous control room stretches out, all shimmery and white and oblong-y.

The boys are running faster. Sarah's mouth has closed, which is a step in the right direction. But she's shaking her head like her puppy tore apart her science project (which Casey had probably built for her, anyway).

A loud pop echoes in the room. Then another. Pop-pop-pop. The alarming sound stops the boys in their tracks.

Only for one second, though.

Tim strides past me so fast that even though my brain says to GRAB HIM, I barely have time to reach one arm out to hook his belt.

My chair whips back around so I have a front row seat while he slaps both of his hands onto a huge pink gelatinous button that is pulsating like a wriggling slug and making rapid fire popping noises.

After one last huge shotgun-like pop, the button shutters down into the control panel.

The sizzle sound abruptly silences.

Everything behind me is still.

Everything in front of me though? Outside the not-window? Moving like crazy.

The tree is gone. The window fills with the blur of blue sky and white clouds and then a flash of brightness and then darkness.

Blackness.

Then stars. Blue, red, colorful stars.

Some getting bigger. All streaking by.

Looking nothing like the nighttime stars I see from the comfort of my bedroom window seat.

It kinda feels like I'm watching from that seat. I don't feel like we're moving at all—it's like I'm viewing the scenery change on a TV set. But I know it's not a movie.

Not the science fiction shows I've crawled inside of all year so I could escape my real life.

Have I finally truly escaped? In the worst way possible?

There's only one conclusion—we've blasted off and are shooting through space. Moving fast away from Earth.

Mouth-hanging-open is definitely an unflattering look

on me. I close it and glare at my reflection in the not-window.

Just this morning I had wished for a way out of my sucktastic eighth grade existence, but now I'd give anything for things to go back to the way they were.

I know.

Be careful what you manifest.

It just might come true.

CHAPTER 2

UNTETHERED, ON AUTO-PILOT, & FALLING DOWN THE EASTER EGG RABBIT HOLE

You'd think my first inclination would be to yell at my brother. Something like, "What on EARTH were you thinking?!" But there are two things I know for sure.

One: If I yelled at my brother for every crazy thing he did, I'd have permanently lost my voice.

And two: We're not on Earth anymore. Outside the window, space stretches farther than anything I've ever seen in my life.

Even when you are out in the middle of the ocean, deep-sea fishing with your dad, you still see a curve on the horizon; the curve that tells you that even though you are on water, you are also still on Earth. That there is solid ground somewhere below you. A reminder that you are tethered to ... something.

Blackness stretches out in front of me now, with no curve in sight.

We are tethered to nothing.

Speeding away from Earth.

I feel an opposite-of-claustrophobic panic coming on. I glance toward Sarah, hoping that she has some calming words of wisdom.

But Sarah's glance-answering shake of her head doesn't pull me out of my panic—an angry red light blinking above my head does.

That red light that makes me think that the autopilot is mostly auto and not enough pilot and is just going to crash us into something sooner rather than later.

Maybe I should drive.

Not that I have my driver's license on Earth—it'll be a few years before I can even consider that. But I'm pretty sure a good-ole PA driver's license wouldn't be recognized to fly in space, anyway.

For a split second, I consider whether NASA gives out rocket licenses. They totally should.

I place my hands (gently) on the control panel to steady myself. The sea of glittery blue and green and pink knobs and dials are making me nauseated, and not just because the saucer has started to pitch.

The red light above my head stops blinking and begins blinking AND screeching.

Aside from a huge curving strip of windshield (and the blinking light), I am surrounded by pastels. The panels around my hands and head are mind-numbing in shades of pink and purple, decorated with buttons and noodles.

Trapped inside a giant Easter egg.

Not my favorite place, which happens to be Geoff's Pizza at the farmer's market. Mostly because the owner (who's not named Geoff) doesn't care if eighth graders hang out on half days, and also because of the lack of brothers, generally, on the premises.

I squint at the blackness rushing past outside, hoping not to see a giant astronaut Easter bunny.

I resist the urge to pull out my phone to find out what is the opposite fear from claustrophobia—no way my phone will work in space.

Stay focused, Kelly, figure out what that blinking light is warning you about. The little niggling voice inside my head has decided to help out, instead of just repeating, *Warning! Danger! Warning!* over and over.

You'd think that my brother and Casey would have tired by now, but you'd be wrong.

They resumed running in oblongs behind me. Yelling loud enough to give that screeching red light a run for its money.

Other people think that my brother Tim is cute, but right now, with his hair streaming out behind him and his face stretched into a look of someone-ended-my-game-without-saving-it-and-now-I-have-to-start-over, or whatever passes for terror in a sixth grader's world, he is anything but cute.

I have to release the autopilot and stop this thing. Turn it back toward Earth and hope that I don't crash into our house.

I wouldn't mind crashing into my nemesis, Jared's house. I mean, as long as he wasn't home, or if he was home, as long as he was only slightly injured. I'm practical —not murderous.

Although, if you knew what Jared did to me at school this year, you'd be telling me to target this Easter egg spaceship directly at his house.

He deserves a big crash.

But I certainly wouldn't want to smash into Sarah and

Casey's house in the process. Even though they are safely on-board with us.

Safely on board? I'm not sure there is anything safe about being inside this thing, although I guess it beats being outside, in space.

Sarah and Casey are our down-the-street neighbors. Sarah's my best friend. I even know her Korean name, that's how close we are—Sun-Young.

I think she should totally go by Sun, because it fits her personality (quiet and shiny), but she thinks Sarah, as a name, is easier to explain to people. She's so quiet, she never wants to have to explain anything to anyone. Even though she has the best nickname ever, built into her name, she won't use it.

I respect her wishes because I'm a great best friend.

Sarah's younger brother, Casey (don't ask me his Korean name—if I ever knew it, I forgot it) is not a completely horrible boy. Even Sarah says so, and she's his sister. That's about as high a compliment as can be paid.

But right now, I can't think through all the hysteria.

So, I yell, "I don't want to crack this egg!" Which, even though it makes perfect sense to me and probably to you as well, seems to stun everyone else into silence.

I shift around on my too-tight seat and nod my thanks to them.

I can't get comfortable, and it's not because our egg is now actively listing to one side. It's because this seat seriously isn't meant for totally normal-sized-human bottoms.

I look at Sarah's huge brown eyes (the white parts bigger than I've ever seen them before) and say, "Have a seat."

As if we are back home at a normal school day in Hillside Middle School's cafeteria.

She does her nervous take-her-hair-out-of-its-pony-tail-and-then-tie-it-back-up before stepping over to the silvery chair next to mine. She puts her hands in the seat and pushes hard. Testing to see if it is sit-worthy. As if I'm not sitting in the exact same thing right here.

I roll my eyes. We're best friends, so I'm allowed.

I know I can't rush her. She won't sit until she's good and ready. She won't do anything until she's good and ready.

So, I stare at the knobs and try to be patient, which is not my thing, and pretend like every second that passes doesn't take us light years, or some equally huge distance away from Earth.

Math's not my thing; all the seconds I normally count to keep my anxiety at bay, have, up until this point occurred in the same time zone, or ... space zone, I guess.

Plus I use an app to calculate those seconds. It's not cheating to use technology, and don't let anyone tell you otherwise.

My brother is making gasping, look-at-me noises behind me, which I ignore. That's practically my default position.

Maybe that seems cruel to you, but if it does, then you either don't have a brother, or your brother is still in the cute-like-a-puppy-dog stage. I swear, there was a time that I thought my brother was cute. Then he grew out of puppy dog and into wolf dog stage.

Actually, that's not being kind enough to wolves.

Sarah re-ties her pony tail one last time and sits down gingerly in the seat.

My ignoring plan seems to work, and Tim shuts up behind me.

Casey, who is more tame-wolf than rabid-wolf, sits down in the seat next to Sarah.

I continue to ignore my brother, who is now tapping me on the shoulder in time to that blaring, blinking light. I want to slap his hand away, but you know; default ignoring mode.

It works, I swear.

"What are we doing here?" asks Sarah.

I look at her with an expression that I hope conveys my astonishment.

I mean, I would think it completely appropriate if *you* asked that question, because you weren't with us one thousand, eight hundred seconds ago when my rabid-wolf of a brother started the Rube-Goldberg-machine-of-bad-choices that ended us on this ship in outer space.

Not everybody is as level headed as I am in an emergency, and moments before, Sarah had been spinning in circles. I should probably cut her some slack.

I slap away Tim's pokey finger and take a deep breath. (Even I can't stay in ignoring mode forever—I told you; patience isn't my strong suit.)

"Hey, Sarah and Casey," (just in case tame-wolf wanted to get in on the saving-our-butts-game), "I'm a bit concerned about this red blinking light. Red is normally a warning, and seeing as how all the other colors here are as cool and pastel-y as ... Easter eggs ... well, we need to figure out what the danger is." I thought I laid out the obvious extremely well.

"But, how can we know what these symbols mean?" Rabid wolf scoots into the chair next to me. He starts turning dials and pushing buttons.

See what I mean?

Crazy.

A novice sister might scream at her little brother when he starts pushing unknown buttons mid-flight in an Easter-egg alien spacecraft. But like I said, I've been his sister for twelve years.

I'm practiced and a pro. I pick up his inquisitive fingers and squash them between my own. Even though I face my brother, I speak to Sarah. "SS ..." (those are her initials), "... we need to find a pattern in the things in front of us. Or figure out what they do—somehow. Not randomly punch buttons."

And, okay, I admit, that last bit came out a bit yell-y and completely directed at Tim. But he is the reason why I am being screamed at by a red blinking light.

Him and his craziness.

I admit, also, that I don't think crazy is always bad, sometimes it's just energy plus creativity plus not enough impulse control.

But rabid-wolf crazy is how we got into this mess, and like heck was I going to let it pull us farther down this Easter-egg space-flying rabbit hole.

CHAPTER 3

STOPPING BY RIGATONI ON A DARK SPACE DAY

I'm sure you don't believe that this is all Tim's fault (although you were with us when he pushed the giant pulsating button that launched us into space, right?!). How could one little brother be that dangerous?

Well, let me tell you.

Eight hundred and forty seconds before we got slurped into this space ship (let's call it bsss—before spaceship slurp) Sarah and I sat peacefully at my kitchen table, still in our pjs, when Tim and Casey came running in and knocked over my Coke.

Yelling about how Tim's toy helicopter landed in the wires behind our house. And, "Sparks, Kelly, sparks!"

Sparks aren't great, I'll grant you that. But they certainly aren't Coke spill-worthy. And, I could tell that my brother's prominent emotion was excitement not fear. He's theatrical that way, so yeah, it's his fault we're here.

He's old enough to know better. To know light-years better.

Now that I've got the noise down to a minimum, I start

trying to figure out what the signs and symbols are on all the knobs and noodles.

And I mean noodles.

That wasn't a Freudian slip because I'm starving—I'm not. My morning grilled cheese was made with huge pieces of yummy Scali bread and will hold me over for a while.

The buttons on the console are soft and gross feeling, like wet spaghetti. Although they aren't long and thin or spaghetti-shaped.

Some are ropey and twisted, like gemelli, some are bigger, like rigatoni, and some are even wheel-shaped like rotelle.

You don't need to look at me strangely, like why does this girl know all the names of obscure pasta?

It's just that for a leaps-before-he-looks kind of crazy boy my brother is, he is oddly specific about his mac 'n' cheese. He'll only eat rotini shaped-pasta. And nothing that I say to him ever convinces him that bow-ties in cheese sauce tastes the exact same.

Like I said: crazy.

I gently feel all the knobs and noodles, careful not to push any. Not yet. Most of the symbols don't make sense to me, but some are arrows. Arrows I understand.

There is one arrow that points backwards, the opposite direction we're headed. And since I want to be traveling in the opposite direction we're going, since I actually wouldn't mind traveling back in time, if it were possible, I take a big breath and push the huge piece of rigatoni above that arrow. I push it hard.

It makes a squelching noise, and we stop.

Completely.

Dead in space.

I jolt in my seat and would fall on the floor except that my butt is wedged in super-tight.

Moving through space felt like nothing, but stopping feels like, well, stopping.

On the control panel, a small screen changes from crude drawings of space stuff—you know, stars, planets, the occasional black hole—to a crude drawing of an oblong space ship.

And I do mean crude—I could draw better than that and sometimes you can't tell my stick-figure people from my stick-figure bunnies. But it looks like it might be a schematic of an Easter egg ship.

Rabid wolf whoops and fist-bumps the air, which has changed from normal see-through air into a kind of wavy, translucent rainbow air.

Sarah, though, mirrors the frown on my face.

See, there's a good reason why we're best friends. It's not some stupid proximity thing, like we're down-the-street-door neighbors, although we are. It's because the same thoughts often occur to her that occur to me. And the current thought that was occurring to me was that it might not be a great thing that we suddenly stopped.

"Push it again, Kel! Maybe we'll go back!" Tim yells between whoops.

I do. I push it again, and nothing happens.

Well, not exactly nothing.

We don't start moving, but on the screen in front of me, a red bullseye appears over the crude schematics of our Easter egg spaceship.

I use the pronoun 'our' loosely. Don't start thinking that I'm becoming endeared to this stupid ship, or that I trust it with our lives. I don't. It's still the enemy we're trapped within.

But I'm also pretty sure that that bullseye means that something bad is happening to our ship.

Something bad is happening to a door on our ship, to be exact.

Because that is where the bullseye lies—over what is clearly a door at the opposite end of the Easter egg.

A blinking bullseye over a door.

The graphic changes and the crude sketch of the door crudely swings open, like a cartoon.

Which, in my mind, means that someone, somehow, is opening up a door on this spaceship, in the middle of space.

I've seen enough sci-fi movies (especially this past year) to know that opening a door in space is not a very good thing.

Sarah and I exchange a glance. See, best friends. Thinking the same thing. That gives me some comfort.

Because no matter what, things are better when your best friend is around.

Both wolves think that the stopping thing was awesome and have settled down.

Which is the only reason why I hear a very quiet whooshing sound, exactly as if air is leaving the egg, and then a metallic clang.

Pretty typical spaceship noises, ones I have heard plenty of times in movies.

But ones that should stay in the movies, in my humble opinion.

I swivel in the shiny, butt-pinching seat, to finally look beyond the rabid wolves, and see that there are five open doors off our main cabin.

According to the drawing on my side screen, there are five doors all around the outside of the ship, and that all doors and corridors dead end where we were—a big oblong cabin.

So, when I start to hear big metallic clunks and those clunks getting louder, I know that whatever just opened the door on our egg in the middle of space, is heading directly for us.

If I were inclined to run screaming in oblongs, now would be the time for it. But I'm not.

I turn back to the controls. I don't know what to do.

Tim starts pushing every noddle in sight, and Casey plants himself on the floor and bangs on the underneath of the console until he exposes the wires on the inside—wires that look remarkably like Earth wires.

I grab Tim's hands off the console. "I don't have enough hands to keep these kids from getting us jettisoned into space," I say to Sarah, who appears to be meditating with her eyes open.

I jab my elbow at Casey, to knock him away from the wires, but he just scoots further away. Tim grunts at the term "kids," but you and I both know I was thinking of calling them something way worse.

"Maybe we should let them try something." Sarah blinks her eyes and bends down to investigate Casey's wires.

She's a lot more tolerant of her rabid-wolf brother than I am of mine, and for good reason—whatever he takes apart, he puts back together eventually. My rabid wolf just leaves destruction in his path.

Case in point: We're on a spaceship, in space, with some clunking THING getting closer.

CHAPTER 4

SOMETHING CLUNKY THIS WAY COMES

So, at seven hundred eighty seconds bsss, my brother spilled my Coke (sooo unfortunate because the fortune on the inside of the Coke can was TODAY YOU WILL GET ATTENTION FROM SOMEONE IMPORTANT, and I was looking forward to seeing if that someone important was Billy grilled-cheese Fowler, but everyone knows that if you spill even a drop of the Coke, the fortune won't come true), and Sarah and I headed outside to save our brothers from themselves, *again*.

But that stupid sparking helicopter was seriously wedged in that wire. Just as surely as we are now stuck on this Easter Egg spaceship.

And those heavy clunks are banging closer. I sit back down.

"How do I make the doors to this cabin close?" I don't think that anyone else will answer, or even really help—I'm used to doing all the important stuff myself.

But I also have a habit of talking to myself, especially during times of stress.

And you know, counting the seconds to ward off panic attacks.

And, yes, in the control room, all five internal doors to five corridors are open. We are inside a huge oblong, wagon wheel, rotelle pasta.

Which is a more accurate description than you can imagine, sitting safely at home with your feet touching flat, solid floor.

Because the floor below me feels a little like pasta—soft and with a little give. Not overcooked pasta, mind you. Perfect, al dente, stick-to-the-ceiling pasta.

Which is probably why the rabid wolf (and the rest of us) didn't break every bone in his body when he tuck-and-rolled into this space ship.

"I don't know. Let's see." Sarah sounds remarkably calm. As if I have asked her to pour me another can of Coke, and she's unsure if we have one in the fridge.

In fact, depending on whether or not she thinks we are out of Cokes, she is a lot more frantic when looking for Cokes than she is right now, scanning the control panel for door closers.

You might think that SS going from running and screaming to suddenly calm is a bit strange. But I've learned that when she's afraid for herself, she's pretty hysterical. When she needs to be strong for someone else, she's a rock.

She's been a rock for me all this year at school.

We sit quietly and scan the control panel. Which is weird. The rabid wolves aren't making noise and their hands aren't randomly pushing and touching stuff.

Maybe we've traveled into some alternate boy-normal universe. The clanking sounds start echoing loud in the cabin and I can feel the sound vibrate through the floor, up my legs and through my sadly-lacking-of-Coke stomach.

"Something's coming, Kelly." Yup, that's my brother, master of the obvious. But sometimes the obvious needs to be stated so it seems okay, or at least like it's truly happening.

Don't mistake my tenderness for actual feelings—he's a rabid wolf and those are pretty hard to love. But, if you want a rabid wolf to calm down and act right, sometimes you have to speak slowly and kindly.

"Yes, Tim. It's coming. But we're all okay and I'm thinking of some plan to get us home. No worries." I smile. Of course, inside I'm all worries. But it's in my immediate interest to keep the rabid wolf calm.

None of the noodles have words that look anything like 'shut all the doors so nefarious things can't get to you and your friend and little brothers on the command deck of an Easter egg spaceship smack dab in the middle of space.'

Not that I can read giant space Easter bunny language. Because, you know, if there is a giant Easter egg spaceship, there's probably giant space bunnies to go with it.

The clunks sound like they are right outside the room. So, I swivel around in my uncomfortable chair and it bites into my hips, on both sides.

I've found that it's always better to look a problem head-on than ignore it. I save the ignoring for my little brother. I plan to face the giant space bunnies head-on.

Everyone else swivels too and I'm feeling pretty proud of all of us, acting remarkably like we belong here, in space. To the outside observer, everything would seem like it's under control in this cabin.

I'm pretty good at pretending—I've had a lot of practice, always pretending like I have everything under control like my classes and taking time off my PR for swim team and my trips to Geoff's pizza and whether or not Billy Fowler knows I exist and how many Cokes are left in the fridge and the chaos of the rabid wolf.

And always pretending that Incident that happened at school doesn't bother me.

I wonder who is outside that door, about to come in and see us looking so good and calm.

The clunks stop just beyond the shadow of the open door.

My brother takes a sharp intake of breath, and I reach over to take his hand.

You know, so my hand will stop shaking.

CHAPTER 5

GOOD TO GOO

So, at about six hundred sixty seconds bsss, one thought saved me. And that thought was, why am I standing out in the backyard with my best friend and some wolves, IN MY PAJAMAS?

I mean, the helicopter making the wires spark, that was dangerous, but I couldn't think of anything more dangerous than being outside in the yard in my pjs in case Billy happened to ride by on his bike.

It was a slim possibility for sure, but my mind was still with my Coke fortune.

I'm an optimist. Even though rabid wolf had spilled my Coke, I was still hoping that my Coke fortune would come true.

I needed it to come true.

If the captain of the boy's basketball team (okay, JV captain) liked me, it would go a long way to making everyone forget about that thing that happened.

Well, maybe not forget, but maybe stop talking about it all the time. I may be an optimist, but after this year, I'm not sure I believe in miracles.

I gestured inside the house, and SS and I ran upstairs to my room,

I stumbled on a stupid remote-control car that Tim must have abandoned on my carpet, and we jumped into shorts and shirts. I may have pulled a brush through my hair as well.

And thank goodness. Because if not, I would be sitting in the control room of an Easter egg space ship waiting for some unknown evil to walk through the door, IN MY PAJAMAS and with medusa hair.

So, thank the Coke Gods for that.

TIM SQUEEZES SO hard that it feels like he is crushing my hand, which I don't mind, since I'm pretty tough. And not in my pajamas.

Whatever has been clunking toward us seems to be waiting just beyond the open door.

I don't know whether to rush forward and try to figure out how to close the door or to invite the thing in, just so we can all stop feeling afraid.

The suspense is killing me.

Soft bangs happen around us, like the ship is cooling down after its retreat from Earth. It sounds like heat pinging through the pipes at home.

And then the noises stop, as if the ship is holding its breath too, waiting for whatever is about to come through that door.

Sarah shoves Casey behind her, and Casey starts pushing wires back into the control panel. As if he's been doing something wrong that he needs to hide before his parents see. A knee-jerk reaction, I'm sure.

Maybe, if we treat it nicely, it won't kill all of us—it's not like we have a chance to fight off anything that can get into a spaceship parked in the middle of space.

And I should probably let it get me first, since my parents would kill me anyway if something bad happened to my brother.

After running through all the logic in my head, I can't stand the silence any more. I'm used to at least one rabid wolf in constant noise and motion around me.

A shadow leaks through the open door.

The owner of the shadow stands right outside.

I drop Tim's hand and open my arms in what I hope is a universal sign for 'I mean you no harm,' and say, "Welcome to our ship."

You know, start from a position of friendly strength.

Tim grabs my left arm, pulls it down, and says (I can't believe HE says it) "Are you crazy, K?"

Because that is what he calls me. Because, he, and most boys, think they are super cool and can make up nicknames for everyone.

The shadow slides into the room, but is more substantial than a shadow normally is—and it changes its shape. The shadow grows and flows out, like a puddle on the floor.

A goo puddle.

Sliding in on top of the goo is a creature that looks like a mashup of Big Bird and an asparagus. All green and stalker-y in the middle, but then plastered in yellow feathers at the top with a bird-like face. It doesn't have legs, and moves by gliding on the wave of goo that precedes it.

You know how people say that humans are really adaptable, well, I can tell you that some are more adaptable than others.

I have been relatively okay with flying in the space ship

—I've at least seen that sort of thing in movies. But for first contact with an alien to be with a giant asparagus bird?

I have to admit my brain sparks out for a bit. Just like the helicopter on the wire this morning.

But rabid wolf's brain seemed to be firing just fine.

"Hey, can I touch that ooze?" Tim scoots out of his seat and walks toward the alien.

I pride myself on being a pretty awesome big sister—I always tell Tim exactly when and exactly what he is doing wrong. But I am still having the sparking-out-brain-problem.

Also, it's not as if he actually waits for answers when he asks permission for something—most of his questions are actually rhetorical.

As if in a dream, I watch my little brother reach down and touch the goo.

"Oh ... K, it's hot! Not like the cheese in your grilled cheese, hot off the sandwich maker, but hot like mac 'n' cheese, ready to eat." Tim grins as he turns toward me.

As if we are doing a fun science experiment.

The asparagus bird waves its wings and its head begins to glow—neon green.

I leap forward and grab my brother's wiggling body and push him behind me.

And the weird thing is that only one thought is in my brain right now.

If this creature slides on goo to move, then what in the name of stuffed-crust pizza was making that clunking foot-step sound?

CHAPTER 6

THANKS FOR THE THANKS

So, five hundred forty seconds bsss (yup, Sarah and I are fast dressers), I ran back into the back yard safely primped in case Billy Fowler rode past.

I cursed my brother (in my head) for always getting us into these messes (and for leaving that remote-control car in my room—I tripped on it again on my way out and nearly plummeted headfirst down the stairs).

The screen door banged behind us, as we ran into the backyard, pulling on our sneakers and Chucks (you know rubber soles to prevent electrocution).

Sarah called to the boys to "Get away from the fireworks!"

Sparks showered down from the electrical wire. If the tree caught on fire, my window sill was very close to a tree branch—the whole house could go up in flames. We needed to stop the sparks.

Were we at the call-the-fire-department stage? I didn't want to be at that stage.

Sisters with calm-wolf brothers might not understand what it means to call the fire department.

But sisters with rabid-wolves know that there are fees and groundings in the wake of calling the fire department for less than life threatening things.

And that a sister's idea of life threatening and a parent's idea of life threatening are two separate things.

Or maybe it's that hindsight is twenty-twenty, and my parents get to play the hindsight card, while I'm always stuck in the moment with the rabid wolf.

The sun roasted the back of my neck as I bent over to grab our hose. Water could be an effective way to stop the sparks and maybe dislodge the helicopter—if I channeled the water with enough force.

I'm not clueless—I know that electricity plus water rarely makes a situation better, but I was fairly certain I could keep everyone away from the sparks and water, and just as certain that I couldn't keep the sparks from igniting the tree right behind our house. So, I weighed the options and turned the spigot on full blast.

I considered blasting my brother first, but I'm pretty decent at self-restraint.

The water turned out to be our downfall. Not because of the sparks, though.

Okay, maybe it *is* slightly my fault that we're trapped here on this spaceship. I was the one to turn on that hose, after all.

But regardless of blame, (and with all his downfalls, rabid wolf isn't the type to point fingers when we have to explain stuff to mom and dad. Oh, no, we're going to have to explain this all to mom and dad!) I don't have long to worry about the clunking because for one, that noise has disappeared, and for two, a booming voice has replaced it.

Weirdly, the voice erupts from speakers on the control panel in front of me. And more weirdly, the voice speaks in Earth English.

"Hello, Captigans! Or that is what I would say if you were Captigans. I am not unaware that you do not resemble Captigans in the least. I am not unhappy at your stupendous rescue! I would give you many thanks if I were to know what you were!"

Casey puts his hand over the speaker on the control panel and pushes the noodle below it. The voice stops, and instead, I hear a quiet birdlike cackling coming from the giant asparagus.

"It's translating! The control panel is translating!" Casey kneels down again and looks through the wires below. That's the problem (one of them) with wolves— they miss the big picture.

"Well, turn it back on then." Tim strides over and slams his fist onto the noodle with a squelching sound.

"... pleasing not to eat you." Says the high, disembodied voice from the speaker.

Again, my brain sparks, and again, Tim steps up. Literally. He walks back to the creature and holds out a hand to shake. "Hello! We are not Captigans, we are Earthlings! Thanks for the thanks—we are happy to help."

As if we did anything to help, at all.

"Well, I do not know that you are not Earthlings, since you are on a Captigan ship, but I know that you are not Captigan since you are unlike any Captigan I have met. Although you drive your ship as skillfully as a Captigan, don't you!"

I'm not going to brag, but I'm pretty decent in English

class which is why I can't understand what in the name of gooey grilled cheese the big asparagus bird is talking about.

Rabid wolf has no such barrier to understanding our alien guest.

He jumps up and down and claps his hands. "Thank you so much for the compliment!" He's in full-on wolf-ambassador mode. "We don't actually know how to drive the ship and would like to go back to Earth. Do you know how we could get there?"

In my surprise, I sit back down into the pinching seat and exchange a glance with SS. A glance that says, who-knew-that-a-rabid-wolf-could-be-so-useful-and-focused? I admit, I didn't know if she got the message, since I don't think I've ever worn that particular look before.

But Sarah's raised eyebrows say back, I-know-maybe-Casey-will-suddenly-become-awesome-as-well.

Although you know as well as I do, that Sarah already thinks that her tame-wolf brother is at least a little awesome. But she does like to offer me sympathy all the time. She's a great friend that way.

While we're locked in our exchanged glances, eyebrow raising and nods, two things happen. Rabid wolf tries to high-five the goo-sliding-big-bird-asparagus, and a green light on the ship's dashboard starts to go berserk.

It starts blinking and buzzing and yelling at us in some language that I don't understand. Why isn't the dashboard translating *that* into English? I don't know. It was probably designed by someone's brother.

But clearly, the asparagus bird does understand. Or he's terribly offended by Tim's attempted high five. "Oh noes and oh yesses. It's not a catastrophe that isn't coming! The not un-Earthlings are not in some serious un-trouble!"

He spins on his sludge and starts high-tailing it out, although he doesn't really have a tail to speak of.

Tim doesn't either, and my mom always says that he's high-tailing it everywhere.

My brain is trying to process all of this new stimulus, but again, Tim is not slowed down by thinking. He jumps in front of the creature and holds out his hands. "Please don't go!"

Casey runs to join Tim in blocking the asparagus big bird's exit, but instead, slips on the track of goo that has slimed up our otherwise pristine and shiny command center.

He bounces onto his butt on the soft floor and slides across the room, skidding on his elbows. His feet hit some big ravioli shaped buttons and immediately big grating metal-on-metal sounds surround us.

My view of the space sky (is it a sky if it is in space? Outer sky maybe?) gets smaller and smaller as a big metal sheet clamps closed outside of the not-window.

The creature slides over to where Casey lies on the floor, and Sarah stifles a scream.

I don't blame her. I wouldn't want some giant asparagus bird running—gliding—after my brother either. Mostly I am bewildered by the alien, but we don't know for certain that he's not dangerous.

In fact, I can count all the things that I know for certain on one hand. These things include: We are all still together, and there is no way that Billy Fowler is going to have any opportunity to pay me any kind of attention today.

Maybe I changed out of my pjs for nothing.

CHAPTER 7

IT TAKES AN ALIEN, I GUESS

At three hundred and sixty seconds bsss, I stood in my back yard, keeping one eye on the water spraying onto the sparking helicopter and one eye out for a cute JV basketball captain on a bike, when something big and invisible swallowed up the helicopter.

Or most of it anyway. I could still see the tail of it, suspended weirdly in the middle of the air, right outside my bedroom window.

And I don't mean to infer that I only like Billy Fowler for how he looks—I'm not shallow like that (most of the time). He is also nice.

And let me tell you, I need to find a guy who is super nice because I know that at some point he'll have to tolerate the rabid wolf, and only super nice guys would still come around when they have to deal with little brothers.

Plus you'd have to be super nice to want to date me after the Incident at school. Billy Fowler has been ultra-nice about that. But that's neither here nor there, and not at all a part of this day—thank goodness.

You might be wondering how I knew that something

swallowed up the helicopter when the something was invisible.

Easy.

The helicopter vanished, but the wires it had tangled up in dipped lower and lower to the ground, like an invisible flock of the biggest birds you'd ever seen suddenly landed on them. Or maybe one HUGE bird. (Maybe a green asparagus space big bird?)

And the water from my hose hit something way up high and rained back toward us. Then one of the wires dipped lower than I had ever seen electrical wires dip and I knew. I knew that now was the time to call in some experts.

But first, we had to get away.

"Get inside!" I dropped the hose and grabbed both wolves by the back of their shirts.

They wore expressions of extreme interest in whatever was bending our wires and the water. You know, curiosity killed the wolf.

But never on my watch.

RIGHT NOW, I grab Tim by the back of the shirt for the second time today, as he tries to run to help Casey.

Sarah is already on the move, and one wolf in danger is much easier to save than two wolves in danger.

Asparagus bird slides to a stop next to Casey. He bends over and pushes the ravioli button with the top of his stalk, and the weird noises around us stop.

Sarah scoops Casey up and slides on the goo herself. If I were trying that save-a-brother-move, I would be on my sore, pinched butt.

But one of the biggest differences between myself and

my best friend is how graceful she is. If I'm walking in the forest I'll trip on roots that aren't anywhere near my feet.

But Sarah could be a dancer (she's not) and doesn't fall. She skids to a stop, landing upright, placing Casey back on his two feet and seems to have a dozen hands as she pats her brother down and smoothes the goo off his back side.

She positions herself between her brother and the asparagus guy.

"That un-silence was not making it un-hard to hear."

I let go of my brother's shirt and try to translate the asparagus's un-English.

In the quiet I notice that the clanging footstep noises have started up again, and they seem to be climbing the walls outside of the control room.

"Oh, no, not again!" The Asparagus Big Bird slides away from Sarah and Casey, across the floor and toward a door on the opposite side of the oblong room. "I'm not un-sorry, but I have to make a not un-rapid leaving of you. It's getting to be too not safe and I'm just not brave enough not to be leaving."

"Wait!" Tim runs over to try to block Asparagus Big Bird's exit once again, but he's not moving fast enough to get in front of the big green stalk. And I never thought I'd see a creature able to move faster than a rabid wolf.

It takes an alien, I guess.

"We don't even know your name!" Of all the things for Tim to be concerned with, of course it is something as stupidly inconsequential as the alien's name.

I'd be happy to come up with a few nicknames and let the asparagus be on his way. We still don't know if he is harmless.

But Tim's statement has a curious effect on the bird. It spins around and makes a circle motion with its thin head and neck. "You are truly not an un-considerate Earthling. I am truly ungrateful not to know you."

The creature continues to slide toward the door, only now it is sliding backwards and bowing to my brother. "If you ever need help of an un-dangerous nature, please call on me."

The clanks seem to come from the ceiling now.

"My name is Franc."

And I know I'm losing my mind. The alien believes rabid wolf to be the be-all-and-end-all of social graces and introduces himself as Franc.

If these things can exist in this galaxy, what, not-on-Earth, will happen next?

CHAPTER 8

SLIGHTLY ELECTROCUTED IS STILL ELECTROCUTED

Remember how I said that it wasn't great that I had turned the hose on the helicopter? And that the water showed us that there was an invisible something landing on our electrical wires outside our house?

Well, that's when everything really started to go south —only we didn't know it just yet.

At one hundred eighty seconds bsss, we ran up the stairs to the top floor of our house—don't ask me why, maybe the basement would have been the optimum choice. But I prefer to be in my own element when dealing with the unknown.

We catapulted ourselves inside my bedroom and shut the door (as if the danger was running up the stairs after us).

Or, that's what I wish had happened. Instead, when we ran into my room, I stepped directly on that stupid remote control car, slid across the room with my arms flailing like a lunatic, and crashed onto the floor.

Sarah did all the graceful stuff, like shutting the door

and shooing the boys to my bed. I collected myself (luckily a basket of not-quite dirty clothes cushioned my fall) and pulled myself up to my window seat.

Wires creaked outside the window.

What I saw wasn't pretty. One by one, the three wires that fed electricity and internet to our house dipped low to the earth, with one snapping, spitting more sparks along an invisible oblong line.

The water hose, which evidently, I hadn't remembered to turn off—I can't think of everything, you know—showered sparks all over our back yard.

If we touched any of that water, we'd get zapped.

I turned back into the room to warn everyone that maybe we should evacuate the house—out the front door, not the back—and call the fire department, but the rabid wolves were busy with Tim's laptop.

"If we lose electricity, there's still enough juice in the laptop to record the images." Casey opened the computer and two images appeared, one of a gooey looking marshmallow field, and one of my butt.

"Does the helicopter have infra-red? Maybe we could see more of whatever is out there?" Tim scooted over to me and grabbed the red car.

The image on the screen changed from my butt to a close-up of the inside of my nose, which was angrily flaring, and spun around the room until it showed Tim's face, looking into the camera, making sure, I guessed, that my klutzy foot hadn't dislodged the spyware.

"What is a car with a camera on it doing in my room?" I didn't wait for an answer. "What is Casey's laptop doing in my room? Do you think you can spy on me and get away with it?"

Right now, you probably think that I threw my brother

out the window and into the spaceship, and I have to admit, the thought did cross my mind.

It took all my focus to stay on target (STAY ON TARGET!). "The water shut off valve is in the basement—I'll be right back."

But I didn't even get a chance to find out why the boys were invading my privacy or to save us all from falling into this spaceship.

WHAT'S CROSSING my mind in this particular second is that I need to somehow gain back some control on this spaceship. I just have no idea how.

The last of Franc's retreating feathers slide out a door on the opposite side of the room, and I hear the clanking just outside another door. We'll call it door number one so there's no confusion about what is happening where.

Sarah inspects Casey more closely, which I guess is another thing that makes her a world of different from me —if that had happened to my brother, not only would we have both fallen on our butts when I tried to rescue him, but I would have been happy that he was standing; not looking for evidence of hurts.

But then again, when you are a sister to a rabid wolf, you have very low expectations.

My job is to keep the wolf alive, not free of bumps and bruises. If you are the sister of a rabid wolf, I bet you know exactly where I am coming from.

But I can't quite tell where those clangs are coming from—the ceiling of the hallway beyond open door number one? That doesn't make much sense to my brain. Less than the existence of Franc, in fact.

Even so, I start to scan the control panel again, looking for a way to cut off the access of that corridor to us.

Tim starts to do the same, only he's running his hand over the control panel, not just his eyes.

That kid can't do anything without touching *everything*.

He'd probably say that he gets to know about stuff by touching everything. I'd tell him he was crazy, and he'd tell me that I was clueless.

Just because I don't touch everything with sticky, messy fingers.

Whatever.

Right now, I am happy we are all still together and still a little mad that the day isn't going to end up with me looking cute while Billy Fowler rides by on his bike.

Or maybe it still can.

All I need is to decide what I am going to do, just like I do every day.

I'm going to close that door, and then take us back to Earth and try to land this Easter egg squarely on Jared's house.

I put my hand back on the backwards arrow button and try to think only of what I'm doing and whether it is a sound choice, but all I can think of is landing this thing on Jared's house and Billy riding his bike past mine.

I know it's totally lame to be thinking of two guys at a time like this, but my brain is on this stupid loop.

I blame the morning's stress.

Speaking of this morning, did I feed Crumbles?

And suddenly my hands are stuck to the control panel. Even my left hand, which had been hovering and touching nothing.

Electricity races up and down my hands and wrists, holding me tight to the controls. But not like Earth electricity—more like warm energy. Alive, cozy, fuzzy electricity runs up and down my lower arms. I can see it—pink lightning bolts—rolling over my hands.

And, you're going to think I'm crazy, but in that moment, and just for a second, I think I hear both Billy and Jared's voices.

The screen that showed the schematic of the ship grays out with static, and then I swear I see the image of a couple of people on that screen. Earthling people.

The fuzzy electricity lets me go, and I wrench myself back.

The schematic is back on the screen, and I look around, trying to decide if those images and sounds really happened, or if I was just electrocuted by the control center.

Both rabid wolves stare at me with confusion in their eyes—did they see the images too? Hear the voices?

Which still doesn't answer my question about electrocution.

But I guess that will have to wait, since I'm not dead, and the clanking outside rises to a fever pitch.

The wolves both turn their attention back to the control panel.

Tim yells out in triumph. "I found the door control!" He raises his fist with a flourish and pumps it onto a spiral shaped noodle button. Resembling more like cellentani pasta, with just a few twists, than gemelli.

I should know—gemelli's my favorite. Not that I get to eat it all that much, since our mom insists on giving in 100-percent-of-the-time to my brother's stupid pasta preference.

I turn back to door number one. I hear metal slide, but door one is still stubbornly open. The whole room shakes with the force of the clunking.

A door *is* sliding shut, but it's door number five—the door that Franc left through. Tim exchanges a look with me, a sheepish-sorry-I-was-over-confident look and then slams his fist down on another spiral pasta button.

I close my eyes as the clanking grows ever louder and when I open them, red light streams in through door number one. Which is now closing, so slowly.

But closing.

Long metal fingers reach around the door and try to halt its progress, but the door wins and closes with a magnificent thump.

We all watch the door—will it hold? And it does.

Clunkings and clankings continue on the other side of it, and I breathe a tremendous breath out.

Did I brush my teeth this morning? I can't quite remember—good thing Billy's not here to check. Although, I think I've been pretty excellent during this whole odyssey; I wouldn't mind Billy seeing me in action.

I sit back down at the controls. Now that the door is closed thanks to my rabid wolf, I focus on goal number two.

Getting back to Earth.

Maybe I should drive.

CHAPTER 9

STUCK STUCK STUCK

At one hundred twenty seconds bsss, while watching sparks flood over an invisible but huge globe outside my window, I felt the grilled cheese start to inch back up my esophagus.

Of course, I wished my Coke hadn't spilled, because we all know that Coke is the best cure for nausea. And headaches, and heartache, and well, most aches.

But my Coke *had* spilled, and unless I found another one on the way to the main water shut-off valve, I was just going to have to swallow breakfast right back down.

Even now, I'm not entirely sure whether I was nauseated by the danger outside the window or the thought that my rabid wolf brother and his friend had been secretly taping me.

Knowing Casey's skill at electronics, they probably had been streaming it live somewhere on the internet.

Had I done anything embarrassing recently? Other than moping around my room, I couldn't think of anything.

Except for getting undressed and into pajamas at the end of each day. Is it possible they taped me naked?

"How long have you been taping me?!" The water shut off valve flew out of my awareness.

Rabid wolf ignored me. He and Casey bent over the laptop. We were in the middle of a crisis, for the love of cheesy bread. Maybe more than one crisis.

They needed to start acting like it. I grabbed the laptop from Casey's hands. "This thing is going out the window if you don't start answering my questions."

Casey's face paled at my words.

But Tim ignored my bluff. "K, something is wrong with the helicopter's camera. I need to get it."

My rabid wolf of a brother walked casually past my bed and opened the window.

Water sprayed in.

You're probably thinking that the reason why the hose was such a bad choice that morning was because water streaming all over the invisible spaceship (because who are we kidding, you've worked out by now that it was the spaceship) and the sparking wires created an electrocution danger to us all.

You'd be wrong.

Electrocution, while it was for sure a danger that morning, wasn't the only danger brought on by that streaming hose full of water.

~

BUT RIGHT NOW, I'm wondering if I finally was electrocuted, not by my foolish water-on-a-sparking-wire stunt, but by the control panel in front of me in this spaceship.

I'm not sure I want to even try to put my hands close enough to the control panel again. I wave my hands over the controls, leaving a safe inch of translucent air in between. I don't feel any buzz of electricity.

Casey ducks back under the control panel and fidgets with the wires under there. Another opportunity for my electrocution.

I could see the gravestone now.

Kelly T.
Coke Fanatic.
Humiliated at school.
Electrocuted in space by rabid wolves.

Tim shoves his body next to Casey's, like he's a mechanic working on the underside of a car.

I hesitantly move my hands back toward the controls.

Driving this thing back to earth is the only option I see —and driving it quickly—before the rabid wolves try something crazy and get us all blown up in space.

Before the clanking thing figures out how to open the door.

Warm pink air grabs my hands and sucks them down onto the control panel again.

I get zapped by the warm fuzzes as if I had just scuffed my feet along a rug and touched our cat.

Images of my spastic tortoiseshell cat, Crumbles, flash through my head. I can almost hear her meowing disdainfully at my brother.

Instinctively, I try to pull my hands off the squishy pasta controls, but the suction is tight.

The buzz vibrates my arms. I try to push the back arrow button again, but my hands are stuck   I can't move them up or down. As if my hands and the control panel are magnets of opposite polarity. I can't push or pull.

Someone whimpers. Me.

Stuck. Stuck. Stuck.

And something with metal hands is still clanking just beyond door number one. More than clanging now. Bangs echo through the control center.

One bang puts a large dent into the door.

Hysterically, that makes me think of that old game show. I rip my hands from the control panel.

"Do you chose what is behind door number one?" Evidently hysteria sometimes makes me say nonsensical things aloud. The stress of the day is exposing some of my weird qualities.

I rub my numb hands together. No way am I putting them back on that control panel.

Sarah settles in beside me and inclines her head. Remember how I said she was super patient?

She clearly thinks there might be some wisdom to what I just said.

I don't know how she is still so calm. Another dent appears in the door. Whatever is on the other side is coming through whether we like it or not.

"I can't touch the controls—they keep zapping me!" I screech at Sarah. I don't know if that's self-apparent, but it seems so since the rabid wolves ignore me and Sarah just nods sympathetically.

Casey moves his hands all the way inside the underneath of the control panel. "Tim, what do these two huge cable remind you of?"

Tim leans back and stares at the ceiling like he's daydreaming at the clouds. Like he has all the time in the world. Like something isn't about to come clanking through the door. Like the only thing that matters right now is some stupid collection of wires. "Hmmm. The parallel processing system of the Joshua 1.0. Do you think there is another center?"

"Another center? Another control center?" Even Sarah seems to understand. I don't know if my brain is short-circuiting from electrocution or from stress. Or if Sarah has gone over to the crazy side.

A huge dent barrels into the door. The Clanker is almost through.

"What are you guys talking about?" I hold up my hand before my brother even starts talking. "The short version, please." I point to the dented door. It looks like it will cave in any second now.

Tim gestures to Casey, and Casey pulls two huge cables out into the room. "This one connects the power source to the control panel. But this one ..." He shakes the cable hard enough that I want to yell at him to drop it. Electrocution danger, you know. "... may connect to a parallel processing center."

"Why do we care about parallel processing?" I barely raise my voice. I'm trying so hard to keep it together. Bangs from the door punctuate each of my words.

Tim speaks slowly, as if I am the child. "There might be a second control center. That seems advantageous to find, doesn't it?" This time he points at the caved in door.

If that clanking sound scared Franc, then I don't want to wait until it is gobbling us down like hot apple crisp with cold french vanilla ice cream on a mild fall day.

"Let's go!" I hop out of my chair and rub my chafed butt. "We'll start with door five," I point to Franc's door, "and go down each hallway systematically."

Yes, let's follow Franc to safety!

"Okay!" Tim jumps over one of Franc's slime trails. He gestures to Casey. "It'll go faster if we split up. Case and I will check out those passageways." He points to two of the five doorways. "You guys check out the other two."

"No!" Can you blame me if I yell, just a little, at this point?

Like blackened-marshmallow-s'mores will I allow my crazy brother to go somewhere on this electrocuting ship without me to protect him.

"We're ALL going through Franc's door." Sometimes you just need to spell things out to rabid wolves.

Something metallic pokes a hole in door one.

"Okay, okay! You don't need to shout."

But we all know that I do.

Tim walks toward Franc's door.

"No way." I grab his shirt to stop him.

Because that's the thing about rabid wolves. They get one success under their belt, and they think they are invincible. Like they have all the answers—to everything. And, sometimes, sure, they luck out.

But sometimes they land you on an Easter Egg spaceship parked in the middle of space with a Clanker trying to kill you and no way home.

We'll proceed with caution.

"Maybe *I* should lead."

I pull my brother behind me and start off through the door.

CHAPTER 10
ALIEN SPACESHIP TURNED BOUNCY HOUSE

Water streamed in my bedroom window at sixty seconds bsss. Before I could scream some safety tip at my brother (you know, like, 'Move your BUTT!'), he reached out and touched the water.

That was the first time that day my heart stopped. Just for a moment (I hoped).

Game over, man. Game. Over.

I waited for sparks to fly out of my brother, his hair stand straight on end, or for him to start convulsing on the floor.

My brother stood normally in the middle of my room. Slightly wetter than normal, but not even remotely electrocuted. "Look at that, no sparks!"

Tim tossed the miniature car back to my bed and took a step *closer* to the window.

The lack of sparks sparked a bad thought into my brother's head. I could see it flash across his eyes. But I was still trying to get my heart to beat again.

Taking care of a rabid wolf is a lot about extinguishing those crazy kinds of sparks. The sparks that said, 'what if,' all day long. Because rabid wolves don't have anything that stops them from acting on a spark after they have one.

Well, my rabid wolf brother did.

I was the thing that stopped him from following his 'what ifs.'

Come to think of it, it was a bit of a miracle we didn't wind up on a spaceship.

Every. Single. Day.

As I TRAIL my hand along the smooth, spaceship corridor, I wonder how much time has passed today—I'm not incredibly hungry, so it can't be too much beyond lunch time.

I pull out my phone, but there is no signal, of course, so there is really no way for me to tell.

I'm getting the feeling that once you've seen one alien spaceship corridor, you've seen them all.

The hallway stretches like a smooth silver hole in front of us, like we're walking in a circular tube, seemingly forever. The yellow running lights on the floor and ceiling remind me of movie theater lights.

In fact, I feel like I'm in a movie. A sci-fi adventure, and I'm that character who always gives the main character the bad news.

Is it a little pathetic that I don't think I'm the star of my own movie? Probably because I spent the year trying to be invisible at school.

Right now, I'd give anything if the running lights grew brighter and some annoying boy told us to 'make sure to take your trash when you leave.' And we would shuffle out of the theater and marvel at how the day grew darker while we were inside.

Like I mentioned before, I saw a lot of movies this year.

But of course, that's not going to happen. And so, I continue to pick one foot up and place it back down on the floor below.

The ground feels less solid each step I take. In fact, it starts to suck my foot in. My fingers sink into the sides as well. The spaceship is beginning to feel softer.

I hear my brother make this discovery behind me and I don't even need to turn to know that he has begun to bounce down the hallway. Acting like it's one big bounce house. Evidently, he thinks it less of a problem than I do.

But that's the curse of the big sister—even when things seem fun, a sister has to give the star of the movie the bad news.

But not yet.

I bend down and push on the floor. It gives, but not all the way.

What's below us? More alien ship? Airless endless space? Scariest environment imaginable? I don't want to find out.

I start walking double time down the corridor. Sarah takes the opportunity of the boys' distraction to catch up to me and whisper her own big-sis concerns.

"Maps doesn't work on my phone—how are we going to find a way back home?"

As if that's the question of the day.

You know I'm feeling stressed when I'm being cranky to my best friend—even if it's just in my thoughts.

We're currently running from some metal alien-thing, and I'm humoring my brother and his friend by pretending to find a safer, parallel control panel so I can what? Get electrocuted trying to fly the ship?

Finding the right direction back to Earth is so far down my list of concerns I can't even think about it.

Although to be fair, when I think of space stretching out in all dimensions from Earth, Sarah has a very intelligent concern. I'm adding it to the list of things to worry about later, though.

The clanking behind us grows softer with every step we take into the green-ish pillow beneath our feet.

I don't like to run blindly from something—I don't like to make decisions based on fear.

But let's be honest—that's what I've been doing all year. Running from something I can't control and can't fix. Living in fear. Afraid of the next time I get a text or go online to check for school assignments.

I guess all I know how to do now is run.

Run, hide in movies and books, and pretend that the bad stuff doesn't exist. Or, at the very least, that there are places where the bad stuff can't find me.

I finally answer her. "I don't know, but we are in a fully functioning space ship that already made it onto Earth once. We just have to figure it out, right?" I pretend that things are okay. I pretend that I'm okay. Just like I have done. All. Year. Long.

I turn back toward the boys so Sarah won't see me wipe the moisture from my eyes.

Tim vaults into the air and does an amazing flip, bouncing onto his feet.

There's some niggling feeling in the back of my mind, like I'm forgetting something on the things to worry about NOW list. Like maybe I'm forgetting the most important thing to worry about right now.

I know better than to focus on trying to figure it out, though.

I relax my mind, letting the thought come to me.

Nothing comes.

Oh well.

I follow the slightly sloping, forever spaceship tube, hoping the thought will come to me.

Or that I'll spot a wardrobe door that says, 'This Way Back To Earth.'

I'd even take Narnia at this point.

CHAPTER II

ELECTROCUTION ISN'T THE WORST THING THAT CAN HAPPEN WITH WATER

So, outside my bedroom window sat what we now know is an invisible oblong Easter egg space ship. But at the time (thirty seconds bsss), all we knew was that something we couldn't see was pushing our wires into the dirt and making the water from our hose stream in weird electric rivers seemingly in the middle of the air.

I can't *really* blame my brother for what he did next, although, of course, you know, I do.

He was just leaping before looking, like he always does.

But the spaceship was wet, and we didn't know how bad a combination that was, yet—a curious brother and a wet spaceship.

~

I TRY NOT to bounce down the hallway.

I don't know if you've ever tried to retain your dignity while walking on a bounce-house floor, but it's not easy.

Even Sarah isn't walking gracefully. We're letting our feet skim the top of the walkway and our knees kick up like we're in a dance-off for the purple power infinity stone.

I try to ignore my brother and Casey flipping around behind us. You know, my default position.

I've composed my face again, after my internal pity party, and am focusing on what is at hand.

A never-ending, ever curving, spaceship corridor.

But the back of my head is still twitching, which is the exact feeling I get when I'm forgetting something.

Something important.

The scary clanking has faded until it becomes dull background noise.

Whatever is trying to get through door number one and into the control room hasn't, yet. And this corridor is blissfully calm. No blinking lights or blaring alarms.

All improvements in our situation.

Still, something gnaws at the back of my mind.

I dismiss it.

It's probably something about home reality.

Maybe I'm late for swim practice or feeding Tim lunch. My internal clock is most likely chugging away.

Sarah grabs my hand so we're now walk-bouncing in sync. She leans into my ear, and I'm careful to keep my head bouncing away from hers so we don't bonk foreheads.

She whispers, "Do you have a plan?"

I take a deep breath.

Luckily twelve years with a rabid wolf has given me poise in strange situations. "One, we'll stay together. Two, we'll stay away from the clanking noise thing, and three, we'll figure out how to drive the ship home."

Sarah gives me a look which clearly states: I-think-you're-crazy-but-you're-my-best-friend-so-I'll-wait-to-formally-pass-judgment.

Which I'm thankful for.

Because if she starts to dig through my plan for holes, we'll all feel worse, instead of just me feeling freaked out about being in charge of everyone's safety.

And there are a ton of holes in my plan. In fact, more holes than plan, I have to admit.

Up ahead the running lights turn a corner. Well, a sloping, round corner. I glance back to see that the boys are now bouncing so high they are bouncing off the rounded ceiling of the corridor. Which seems pretty typical of rabid wolves, but also tells me that maybe the hallway is getting bouncier, if that's possible.

My knee almost hit my nose as I slide forward.

I'm not sure what this means, but the twitching is becoming more of a jerking in the back of my mind.

What on not-Earth am I forgetting?

I turn the corner, still holding Sarah's hand. Which makes me think of Billy.

I love SS, but if I had my druthers, I'd be holding Billy's hand right now.

With all that's happened at school, it's weird that Billy has even given me the time of day. But it's not all in my head—everyone says he's really seemed interested in me recently.

Even my nemesis Jared mentioned it teasingly last Friday. Now, don't think I let Jared talk to me—I don't. I always walk away.

My face turns red and I hope that the yellow lights are too dim so Sarah can't see. She gets really upset when I think about Jared and what he's done to me this year at school.

The color of the corridor beneath my hand is changing slightly. It's no longer silvery-white, but an iridescent blue, and it is turning a darker shade of green where the yellow lights hit it on the floor.

I had expected to find the door to another room or a fork in the hallway by now, but it's been smooth and one dimensional.

What if this corridor leads us all the way around the perimeter of the spaceship and into door number one? We'd meet the Clanker for sure.

Unless it's following us.

We'll just go in endless oblongs on this spaceship until we can't walk—bounce—anymore.

My left foot sinks so far into the floor that I have to wrench hard to get it out.

Squinching noises happen all around us as if our feet are suctioning into the floor.

Sarah's hand tightens her grip on mine, and her face turns white.

This is not. Good.

"Turn around. Go back." I bark out the orders.

Wheeling around to face the boys, I pull Sarah with me. Something drips down my cheek, and if it wasn't ice cold, I might think I was crying.

But I'm not crying.

I look up. Drips of water, like condensation, line the top of the corridor and drip off. Some borrow the color of the lights up there, and shine like yellow rain. It's not acid. It's not harming us. But my heart starts thumping anyway.

That niggle is holding a drum parade in the back of my mind, which is not helpful at all.

I am not forgetting swim practice. Or lunch. My stomach grumbles. Okay, I could handle another grilled cheese. But that's not the thing I'm forgetting. (I couldn't possibly forget grilled cheese, anyway.)

I flash back to standing in my bedroom at two seconds bsss, and yelling at my brother, "DON'T REACH FOR THAT HELICOPTER TAIL." And, "DON'T LEAN THAT FAR OUT!"

But I was too late.

He leaned, I held onto him, but couldn't keep my balance, and we fell.

Out the window and through the wall of the wet spaceship.

Fell isn't really the right word—he got slurped in. And of course, I was holding his shorts and got slurped in after him.

And the next thing I knew, we were in the control room of an Easter egg spaceship and my best friend and her brother were slurping through after us.

Something about water sucked us through the shell of this Easter egg.

And now the corridor floor I'm standing on is sopping wet.

And so is the floor my brother is standing on.

"Tim, GET BACK."

But it's too late.

I grab for his arms as he gets slurped through the floor of the spaceship.

I miss.

He falls.

CHAPTER 12

SLURPING THROUGH SPACE

As always where my brother is concerned, I have mere fractions of seconds to make a split decision. Now you know how we ended up on the Easter egg ship, and I have to guess you know what I do next.

As if it is even a decision.

It's really my default mode. I always follow after my crazy-doesn't-look-before-he-leaps brother.

"Tim!" And then I jump as hard as I can onto the floor where he just disappeared.

As I slurp through the wet, satiny floor, I hope to the Coke Gods that I'm not falling out into space. I guess that would be over before I knew it, which would be something.

I lock eyes onto Sarah as I fall. "Don't follow me!"

I mean to say so much more, but she disappears and I land on a rather lumpy floor.

A moving, lumpy, boney floor. I sit up on Tim's stomach and roll off of him as quickly as possible.

He helps me out with a hard shove.

He's great like that.

A blur falls from the ceiling and Casey nails Tim in the side with his shoes.

I yank them both to the side as Sarah gracefully lands on her two feet. She's like a cat, my best friend.

"I told you NOT to follow me."

Sarah rolls her eyes at me, and I roll mine back.

I don't know how to get everyone else to figure out that this isn't a fun space adventure, but a matter of life or death.

Sure, we fell into another corridor on the ship, looking remarkably exactly like the one we were just in, but we could have fallen out into space.

On the other hand, I also don't want to freak everyone out.

Water follows us down from above, and I can already feel the floor beneath my feet soften.

"Let's move." I point in the direction that would be back toward the control room, if we were still on its level.

This corridor mirrors the one we fell from, except that instead of a silvery color, this corridor is a warm golden color.

I push Tim and Casey in front of me and catch a really annoying shared grin between the two of them. Yup. A space adventure. That's not going to help us get home—them thinking this is fun and games.

"Get moving, you two." Like I'm a drill sergeant making them march.

I tune them out as they start talking about how awesome it was to fall through the ceiling.

As if.

I put both hands out to check the solidness of the walls. Sarah puts her hand on my shoulder, like she's blind and I'm leading us to safety.

The walls suddenly feel like they are closing in.

But that's in my head. And I can't lose it right now. I have to stay calm for my brother. For Sarah. For Casey.

I take a deep breath.

The corridor feels hard to the touch and isn't actually closing in.

I repeat the breath even though I just want to freak out. I touch the part of my chest that hides my heart. Try to count. One two three. Breath in. One two three. Push the air out. The haze in my head recedes.

I take stock.

I wish I didn't have to be the drill sergeant today. More than anything, I wish I was back in my yellow kitchen, checking out the fortune inside my Coke can and enjoying the endless possibilities of the day.

I didn't expect actual endless possibilities.

"I wish my Coke hadn't spilled. I wish my fortune had come true—that I did get attention from someone important. There's no way that I can get attention from Billy up here on this stupid spaceship."

Sarah sighs beside me. She's all girly like that. She sighs. And sometimes, she cries. I can say that about her because I'm her best friend.

But her sighing also means that I just said that stupid thing about my Coke fortune out loud. I hope I didn't say the other stuff I was thinking—that there is no way that Billy actually likes me   that I'm completely undatable.

The lights lining the floor and ceiling of the spaceship start blinking.

Who knows if that is normal?

Not me.

I'm on a spaceship, and I'm thinking about a boy? Something is wrong with me.

Since the wall seems super strong and not at all fall-through-able, I grab Sarah's hand.

"Billy's cute and all, but he's a little predictable. You need someone surprising and awesome." It's not the first time Sarah has said something like that.

So, I respond as if I'm reading from our normal script. "I need someone solid and dependable and nice in my life! I have too much adventure already with rabid—I mean, Tim."

I try to be nicer to my brother in my spoken words than I am in my thoughts. It's my grand plan to help him be more normal. You know, fake it until you make it.

I fake that he's normal until he is able to make it.

I'm not entirely sure it's actually working.

We are ON A SPACESHIP, after all.

I reign in the impulse to kick his little, self-assured butt wiggling in front of me.

"Plus, it's not like beggars can be choosers. I'm lucky any boy will give me the time of day right now. Billy's a catch. For me."

I nudge Tim to get him moving a big faster.

Sarah sighs again. Because as my best friend, her job is to care deeply about my love life. Nonexistent as it might be.

The blinking lights around us blink out. Leaving us in pitch blackness.

I trip over a wolf's feet, and fall to the corridor's floor. I'm weirdly happy that the fall hurts; the floor is hard beneath me.

"Kelly?"

"Here."

Sarah grabs me by my awesome black belt that is looped cutely through my shorts and hauls me to my feet.

She pulls me into a quick hug and we stand in the dark and try not to freak out.

"Kelly?" Tim's voice sounds tiny and helpless. Like his humor and go-with-the-flow-ness has turned off with the light.

"It's okay, bud." I reach out and pull someone toward me. It turns out to be Casey, but he pulls Tim with him.

We huddle together, like we're about to snap a football. Football's not my sport.

I hear drips behind us, but otherwise the silence is unnerving.

The hum of machinery that I didn't realize was constant until this very moment is gone.

I focus on our breathing and try to figure out the next step.

Regardless of pitch blackness, we are all together. We'll wait a moment to see if the lights come back on.

Another sound bursts into existence behind us. It's not the reassuring sound of engines running. Shivers go up and down my spine like those sparks flying this morning in our back yard. A clank bangs behind us. And another. Moving closer to us.

Casey whimpers and Tim breaths my name so quietly it sounds like a prayer.

"GO. Get away from the Clanker!" I give Tim a gentle push.

The clanks grow louder, heading our way.

CHAPTER 13

THINGS IMPROVE AND THEN DON'T

Done of us are walking down the hallway. We're banging down the hallway.

I'm bouncing into Tim's heels—or maybe Casey's too, I can't see— and then into Sarah and then into the wall.

Which means I'm consistently banging my head. The corridor curves back toward the ceiling just at my head's height.

Sarah is softer than the wall to bang into, but I know each time I bump into her, she bumps her head into the far side of the wall.

There's some math idea about that—opposites attract? No—every action has an equal and opposite reaction. Eat that, Mrs. Swimple. I knew I deserved a better grade than I got in math last semester.

The clanks follow us steadily down the dark hallway.

I ricochet off Tim, onto Sarah, and then into the wall again. My head hits hard. And this time, it doesn't feel like a smooth wall. I hit the corner of something.

"Stop!" I grab the profusion I hit my head on, and try to

feel what it is with my fingers. "Everyone, there's something here."

"I don't care—I don't want to meet whatever is making that noise." Casey is normally quite brave—I mean, he has to be to follow Tim into all those crazy schemes. But I can't blame him. In the dark, I'm scared too.

And the clanks keep coming.

Sarah whispers, "Lumos," and a light blinds me.

It takes a second for my eyes to adjust. Sarah shrugs in the light of her iPhone. I shrug back. Not sure why it didn't occur to me to use the flashlight on my phone. It's probably the only app that is useful in space.

Sarah shines the light at my fingers. It only takes a second to recognize the thing that hit my head as a door hinge.

As if the four of us are all of one mind (Coke-forbid I ever share a mind with a rabid wolf) we back up.

There's no handle. The wall is completely flat. No evidence of a seam or break in the wall. In fact, the hinge seems to blend in with the door now that we aren't looking straight at it. We never would have found it if I hadn't banged it with my head.

Not that finding a door hinge is very useful. Especially if there's no way to open the door.

The clanks stop for a second.

Which gives me a moment to pause and take stock.

But of course, rabid wolf can't pause. He pushes and pounds and presses all over the area around the hinge.

Casey swallows something large (probably his fear) and nods. "Well, we haven't seen any sign of that cable since we've been in the corridor—it must weave through the walls and into the inner rooms."

Which just seems to make my rabid wolf brother push and shove more things around the hinge.

He's going to get us killed.

I put my hands to my face and rub, hard.

I want to yell. Yelling will not help. Yelling will not help at all. I let go of my forehead and grab his hands. I don't mean to be rough, but there you go.

"Wait. I felt something. There." Tim wriggles out of my grasp and pushes his fingers *through* the door.

Tim grins big in the glow of the iPhone. He looks eerie. Like a jack-o-lantern, or a spooky storyteller at the edge of a campfire.

The lights blink back on around us, and the clanks start up again.

I pull Tim's hand out of the wasn't-even-there-a-moment-ago hole in the wall. But instead of pulling his hand free, the wall comes with him.

Of course, he's holding on to the wall as I pull.

And it's not a wall, but a door. He's figured out how to open a door in the wall of the spaceship's corridor.

Without pausing for a moment, without even looking inside, Tim goes through the door. Casey follows him. Sarah follows, holding onto Casey's shirt.

I roll my eyes. Hard.

What is so wrong with looking BEFORE you leap?

I lean against the wall. My brain feels tired. I don't want to see any more new alien stuff. My usual cure for tired is another Coke. If only.

The clanks are now so close that I might be the crazy one for standing in this hallway.

But you know when you've reached as much as you think you can handle? That's where I am right now.

Standing alone in the corridor with no grilled cheese or Coke in my foreseeable future.

I turn toward the clanks but someone grabs my shirt and pulls me through the open door.

I only get a quick glimpse of metal in the hallway behind us as the door closes behind me.

CHAPTER 14
ALIEN SPACE TV IS WEIRDER THAN FRANC

I blink my eyes into focus in a bright cavernous space, almost as big and circular as the control room above. The floor seems solid—for now.

I turn to my best friend. "Thanks, Sarah." I love having a best friend who always has my back. Literally, this time.

"That wasn't me that pulled you in—that was Tim." Sarah hugs me to her, and I turn around to lean on the now-closed door.

Even rabid wolves luck out and do the right thing every once in a while.

I don't mean to diminish his actions, though, and you know I'm training him up to be less rabid.

I nod my thanks to him, but he's moved on to something more interesting than me.

See, so rabid.

The room we're in is like the control room, except that there's no space to run oblongs in it—it's filled with stuff. Not just any stuff. It's filled with blinking and beeping machines.

Every inch of the machines are covered with dials and

buttons and levers and more. My absolute worst nightmare of a place to be trapped in with my brother who can't keep his hands to himself.

Or is it?

Upstairs in the control room, he figured out how to close the door when we needed it closed. And just now he saved me from whatever is clanking down the hall.

But he also got us into this mess.

Yup. Still my worst nightmare.

I turn to the door and listen for the clanking. I can't hear it. Which probably means that the door and walls in this room are sound proof.

Which makes perfect sense; from the hallway I didn't hear any of these machines. Now I can't hear the clanking. But we have to assume that whatever was clanking is waiting for us outside that door.

But I'm so hoping it just clanks right past.

I walk my fingers over the door—or what I think is the door. I can't find any sort of lock. I can feel where the wall gets soft. My fingers slide into it in the same spot as where Tim's hand went through. It feels like I'm sinking my fingers into marshmallows, only without any stickiness.

I pull my hand out. No lock. And I don't want to accidentally open the door—no way.

Even with my back to rabid wolf, I know he's touching stuff.

"Don't touch ANYTHING." I wheel around and give up on the door. I have more pressing issues than trying to lock it.

Rabid wolf looks over his shoulder at me but doesn't stop his fingers from exploring every inch of a huge metal box that looks like a refrigerator but with grooves and buttons and wires all over it.

"What fun would that be?" Tim moves onto the next beeping thing, which resembles an air conditioner.

I throw my hands into the air. Yup, like cartoon characters do in Loony Tunes. Come to think of it, I'm feeling a bit looney.

I ball my hands and then open them up like they are blinking my words at Tim. "This. Isn't. Supposed. To. Be. Fun."

Sarah grabs my waist and pulls me into her, like we're doing a weird intergalactic jig, complete with hip bumps. We bounce a little on the not-entirely-hard floor.

Sarah is much more tolerant of rabid wolves. She wants me to be more tolerant too. I can see it in her earnest eyes.

I mentioned that SS is quiet. I didn't mention how extremely quiet she actually is, because I really want you to like her. Really shy people can seem standoffish, but she doesn't have a judgmental bone in her body.

I find her silence refreshing. After a moment focusing on her, I feel much more zen and less like I want to pound on my brother. Well, a little less, anyway.

I still want to stop his little fingers from touching every blinking button in this blinking room.

I stride over to rabid wolf and pull him to face me. With my hands on his arms, I try to hold him still like I'm his straight jacket.

His gaze darts back to the huge air conditioning-like unit next to us.

"Tim. Look at me."

Instead, his gaze runs around the room, and I have to pick my battles. "When you touch everything without knowing what might happen, something might eject us into space."

His gaze wanders back to me.

I know it's a lost cause.

His eyes fill with feverish excitement. Nothing I can say will make a dent in him feeling like this is a big old ice-cream-sundae-with-gummy-bears-on-top adventure.

I sag to the side and release him to his own devices.

Maybe there is a Coke in that machine that looks like a refrigerator.

Even though I'm joking to myself, I wander over. I might as well make the most of things. I glance back over at rabid wolf, and my hands itch to squash his fingers again.

We need to leave this room before Tim does something we can't come back from.

Sarah pops up right in front of the giant fridge.

"So, one: Stay together. Check. Two: Keep safe from the thing in the hallway, check. Three: Find out how to fly this thing home. Let's work on that one." She's trying to distract me from my brother's craziness.

I don't think it's working.

I spin around in place. No second control panel. No how-to-fly-this-Easter-egg-without-frying-your-brain manual in sight. Believe it or not, I'm walking on air.

But there is a hatch in the fridge in front of me. I point to it and Sarah moves out of the way.

I ignore the wolves' happy chatter behind me. Discussing whether that big cable led to this room.

I'd love a Coke.

I push all around the hatch until something gives and the door, no bigger than a bread box, swings open. Inside sits a static-filled TV screen.

My hand flies to my mouth in surprise. Maybe to keep me from uttering anything at all until I understand what I am seeing.

Most of the screen is filled with static, but the parts that aren't, the parts that grow clear and then melt back into static, those parts hold the image of two spitting-mad boys. And an occasional jumping cat with claws bared.

I am watching my crush, Billy, and my nemesis, Jared, yell at each other on a TV screen on a spaceship in the middle of space. Oh, and my cat, Crumbles, looking a bit like a rabid wolf herself.

Rabid wolf sidles up to me. "Wow. Now THAT's cool."

CHAPTER 15

REALLY?! MY COKE FORTUNE CAME TRUE?

Now, I'm not ugly. And I'm not knock-down gorgeous. I'm girl-next-door-cute, and it doesn't make me vain to say so.

Back at Hillside Middle School's cafeteria, it's not like I'm turning heads, though. Especially since the incident. I've been what you could call un-dateable.

So, when the two boys that I've been thinking about all morning (believe me when I tell you that I wish I could keep myself from wasting a second on thoughts of Jared) show up in a TV screen yelling at one another, my first thought isn't that they are somewhere in the galaxy fighting over me.

That's more like my second thought.

But, anyway, my FIRST thought is that the machine is wired telepathically to my thoughts, and that I am thinking about the boys arguing and that is what is being transferred to the machine.

Let me remind you, I am on a spaceship. Weird things are possible. Well, probable.

But it's not like I am really thinking about them fighting about me.

I mean, I don't know if Billy actually likes me—even though he does ride his bike past my house an awful lot.

And I'm not even going to talk about Jared. End of discussion.

So it can't be a manifestation of something from my mind.

And even though I'd love for Billy to be defending my honor, they probably aren't fighting over me.

Remember, I'm not the main character. I'm the person who has to say things like, "I'm reading it right; they're in the room with us," when the aliens arrive. And then I'd get killed if this was a movie.

But it does seems like they are fighting over something.

Sarah has her brow furled like she does when she's calculating how long the shelf full of Cokes will last us and how long before she and I need to pool our allowances to buy more.

My mom says that if I want to fill my body with chemicals, then I have to do it on my (and Sarah's) own dime.

Sarah doesn't understand the same thing I don't understand—which is really everything about why two guys I was just thinking about are now on TV in space.

Too bad it is only video with no audio.

Out of big-sister-habit, I turn to check on the boys.

Tim, of course, is enthralled by the spectacle on the screen in front of us. There's nothing more interesting to a younger sibling than ANYTHING relating to their older sibling's love life.

Casey peruses the room behind us, not stricken by rabid wolf's must-fiddle-with-everything-itis, and probably still looking for his huge cable, so I turn my attention back to the weirdness in front of me.

"What are they doing there?" Sarah reaches forward to touch the screen.

I don't have an answer. Maybe it's rhetorical.

Tim walks around the box like everyone does on Doctor Who. I'm pretty sure this box isn't bigger on the inside, but what do I know?

This morning I was pretty sure I wasn't going to be launched into space.

I realize I'm no longer feeling like I'm going to lose my mind or punch my brother, which is weird, since things have only gotten more bizarre and crazy-making in the last few moments. But hey, I'm not one to look a gift horse in the mouth.

Rabid wolf picks up a huge ribbon of wires and follows it away from the box.

I want to yell, *Danger, Will Robinson, danger!* Hmm. Maybe I'm not feeling more sane after all. My brain seems to be mashing up all the sci-fi shows I've ever seen to process the insanity around me.

And like I said, I've seen a lot of TV shows and movies this year. When you're a social outcast, and even the swim team is keeping a bit of a distance, you escape however you can.

I leave Sarah pushing on the TV screen and walk as calmly as I can to the rabid wolf.

It's my turn to fake it until I make it. I need to pretend to be in control of the situation so I don't have to face the fact that I'm going crazy.

"Why are you holding alien wires in your human hands?" Yup, I hear myself sounding pretty darn looney-tunes.

"I want to find out where they lead." Tim winds around machines and steps over other bundles of wires lining the floor.

"Wires coming from electrical things generally lead to the power source. Why do you want to find the power source?" I can't believe I'm following my brother like a little puppy right now.

So much so that I bump into him when he stops short.

"Here." He hands me a wire, and I take it. Yup, totally crazy. "Follow this one over that way. I'll follow this big bunch."

Without waiting to see if I agree, Tim follows most of the wires toward a corner of the vast room. I look at the pink wire in my hand, note that it is shaped just like a huge strand of gemilli pasta and start following it as it branches to the left. I am thankful it doesn't feel like pasta, like everything else does on this spaceship.

So gross.

I walk all the way to the edge of the room, stepping over other pastel wires until I reach a large white wall into which that the pink gemelli wire disappears.

"Come here and see THIS!" Even if I didn't spend way too much time with rabid wolf, I would recognize his Eureka voice.

I let go of the pink gemelli and race over to Tim. He doesn't always understand what is Eureka-fun and Eureka-dangerous.

Garter snake in the river behind our house; Eureka-fun. Raccoon walking drunkenly through our front yard in the middle of the day; Eureka-dangerous. That time, I threw our recycling bin over it and called pet control.

I don't know who to call in the middle of a spaceship. Who do you call? Ghost Busters!

I'm definitely losing it.

When I reach Tim's side, I see that all of the rest of the wires (which mostly look like standard spaghetti) feed into a side of the wall exactly like the walls of the corridor outside. Only these walls curve out, like a bubble protruding into the room.

From beyond the white bubble wall, I hear the unmistakable, if severely hushed, sounds of two boys arguing almost to the fist-fighting stage. And the crows and spits of an extremely angry cat.

If I'm not losing my mind, and I have to admit, that's a distinct possibility, Billy and Jared are INSIDE this spaceship with us.

And they don't sound happy about it.

At all.

CHAPTER 16

SOMEHOW THERE ARE TWO MORE RABID WOLVES AND ONE SPITTING CAT ABOARD

It's entirely impossible to look cute while doing certain activities. My mind goes back to Casey's laptop in my room. What private things did I do while the rabid wolves were taping with that stupid remote-control car? Lots of un-cute things, I'm sure.

Maybe the universe is out to make my year the most socially damaging in the history of history.

Nobody looks cute while arguing.

I remind myself of that as I walk back to the fuzzed-out TV screen.

"They're heeere." I sing-song to Sarah and make a mental note to stop watching so many movies.

"Who's here?" She asks. She watches her brother explore the room's wires without putting his hands all over everything. See, tame wolf.

I point to Billy's pixelated almost-frothing face which seems really out-of-character for him. I've only ever seen him being nice.

I swear Jared rolls his eyes—of course HE can't take anything seriously.

"Wait, what?" Sarah's eyes widen. "Here?" She gracefully taps the spaceship floor with her toe.

I nod my chin over toward the corner with the big white wall bump and Tim walking his hands over it like he's a mime. Looking for a door handle-hole, I imagine.

"They're HERE?" Sarah turns on her heels and heads over to Tim, calling Casey along the way. Of course, he immediately stops what he's doing and follows her.

So tame. Not gonna lie, I'm a little jealous.

I detour over to the door we came through, listening for clanks.

I put my ear up to it—nothing.

Everyone else clusters around the smooth white bump, but I need a moment.

I admit I'm stalling. But you might too—there's only so much crazy a practical person can handle. Even a practical person who has been practicing with the crazy of the daily ins and outs with her rabid wolf brother.

I mean, I pride myself on being able to deal with the crazy. That's my job.

Well, I've been hinting to my parents that I want to get a job at Geoff's pizza but right now if I asked outright, I can tell the answer would be no. I'm warming them up to the idea.

So, it's my unofficial job as big-sis to deal with the crazies right now. And I'm good at it. That's not braggy— that's the truth.

All the blinking lights and spinning machine parts in this room start to give me a headache. My brain is always tuned in to tracking movement, rabid wolf style, and there's no break from moving parts in this room.

I lean in to the wall and enjoy how it feels. Hard, stable, but not like walls back home. More like Model Magic after it's dried overnight. Soft, but also hard.

Maybe Tim is wearing off on me—I'm totally enjoying the impossible nature of the spaceship walls.

Rabid wolf slides into me. "Kelly, I can't find a door handle to let them out. Come help." He grabs my arm and tugs.

I resist. I'm not done having my quiet moment. My head throbs. I press my shoulders into the wall and try to relax.

The truth is that the last thing I want is to let Jared out of his jail. He deserves it in there.

Rabid wolf tugs again. "What if there's only a little air left in there?"

You know I like to give proper credit when it's due, but I'm a little unnerved that rabid wolf got to the big picture problem before I did.

I have several default positions; some I've already told you about. Planning my day and weighing the pros and cons is one, ignoring my brother is another. Following my brother to dig him out of trouble is a third. My fourth default position is thinking about the worst thing that can happen and then preventing it.

So far, I haven't been able to ignore my brother or plan my way off this spaceship. And I totally missed the worst thing that could happen right now.

I'm seriously off my game.

Stupid Easter egg spaceship getting the best of me. No way would I take that sitting down. Or leaning against a wall that is simultaneously hard and soft.

We have to get my cat and Billy out of the cell-like room. If Jared happens to escape too, I'll just have to live with that. This Easter-egg spaceship doesn't seem big enough for me to avoid him.

I shake loose from Tim's hand and propel myself off the wall.

"So, let's look at what we know about this wall material." As I walk to the wall bump, I smile at Sarah. Her face relaxes from a worried frown into a slightly less worried frown.

"It's hard and soft at the same time." I think of that feeling of model magic.

Rabid wolf is literally running circles around me. "There are sometimes holes for door handles," Tim says.

"It's smooth all the way around," Casey chimes in. Clearly not as vital information as Tim's, but not everyone can get to the essence of things the way a rabid wolf can.

Credit.

"Any luck in finding a door handle, Tim?" Obviously I know he hasn't, otherwise there would be two fighting guys out here rather than in there.

I'm close enough now to hear muffled yells. It must be terribly claustrophobic in there. Sarah's face blanches as she reaches the same conclusion.

I hope the air isn't getting stale. As long as I can hear the voices, I know they're still okay.

"Merow!" Crumbles yells.

Tim starts miming his hands all over the surface again. "I've touched every square inch—can't find anything that feels like the door handle-hole did."

I survey the blinking machines humming around the room. "SS, you and Casey look for a machine that might open this wall."

Sarah narrows her eyes at me.

Remember how she wouldn't sit in the chair before she

knew it was one-hundred-percent safe? Well, asking her to do something without knowing the outcome makes her nervous. Eat-her-hair nervous.

She starts to nibble on it as she walks away. We all have to step up right now. Sarah too. But I feel bad. She's my best friend.

I put my hands on the curved wall. Soft and hard. Also weirdly warm. I'm still thinking of Sarah being out of her comfort zone, so I ignore that thing in the back of the head that tells me I'm missing something.

I really have to stop ignoring that.

And maybe I should give it a name. I'll call it Annoying Niggle. Because that's what it feels like.

So Annoying Niggle pokes at my mind while I push my fingers all over the wall, reaching up higher than my brother.

I hear the muffled arguing from inside—reassuring. I don't hear any clanking out in the hallway—relieving. Water dripping inside this room—Annoying Niggle.

WATER DRIPPING!

Water dripping, somewhere behind me in this room.

I whip around just in time to see a medium-sized steel cabinet fall through the floor on the opposite side of the room. Water drips down from the ceiling above where it used to be.

I scan the entire ceiling. On the far side of the room, the ceiling is a blueish hue. Beads of water gather all the way from that side into the middle of the ceiling, moving toward us. Sarah and Casey are frozen, halfway between Tim and me and the lost cabinet. Droplets form above their heads.

"Get back here, guys. It's wet. We need to get out before we fall through the floor!"

I hear the muffled arguing continue—don't boys ever

get tired? I can't leave Billy and Jared trapped in their cell. In the back of my head, Annoying Niggle tells me it's probably my fault they are here. Somehow.

Shut it, Annoying Niggle.

But if we stay, there is a good probability we will all fall out of the ship and into outer space.

I grab my brother's hand.

It is time. Time to unleash the rabid wolf.

"I'm out of ideas. Tim, what do you have?"

He grins like the Cheshire Cat, even though that movie hits a little too close to home right now. Falling through a hole and into a new world?

A world I'd give anything to fall back out of.

Another machine falls through on the other side of the room.

A drop of water hits my face.

I don't want to freak Tim out, but we're running out of time.

CHAPTER 17

RABID WOLVES & ANNOYING NIGGLES & NEMESES, OH MY

You know when you are sitting at your favorite pizza place, sipping your Coke, and you hear the sound of your brother's voice come through the door, and you know that your day is ruined? That all your afternoon plans are kaput because now your only purpose in life is to keep someone out of trouble who excels only at getting into it?

Maybe I'm taking a leaf out of Franc's book right now, because hearing Tim's voice is giving me the opposite feeling.

"We'll figure it out, K. We won't fall." Since when does rabid wolf reassure me?

But, boy do I need some reassuring.

Across the room from us, water slides from the ceiling in streams now.

Machine start to sink into the floor. And then another one pops through. Wires from it pull tight and then break off, and for the second time today I'm seeing sparks before my eyes.

"You guys go. Find the door and go. I'll get Billy and

Jared out." Even as I'm speaking the words, Sarah and Tim shake their heads 'no.' Although when Tim shakes his head his whole body gets in on the action. Like a dog, or a tame wolf. Because rabid wolves don't try to save their sisters.

Credit.

Rabid wolves don't try to save anyone.

Banging noises from inside the wall bubble focuses me back on the task at hand. No room for getting all sentimental up in this Easter egg spaceship.

Another machine falls through the floor, and Tim yells, "Jump!"

Wires slide across the floor after it, and we all jump like we're in the back yard playing double-Dutch. What's next? Hopscotch?

Limbo is actually next. Wires pull tight and raise up three feet off the floor. The machine must be dangling from the wires, which are still attached to the wall behind us.

Sarah and Tim are on one side. Casey and I are on the other. I push Casey under and scoot after him.

The wire pulls from the wall and throws sparks past us. Tim grabs his arm in pain.

"Let me see it." I turn his arm over. His shirt is smoldering, so I pull it over his head and off him.

"Hey." Tim tries to cover his naked chest with his elbows, while I inspect his arm. There's a pretty serious red spot, but it's not too bad. I make sure that the shirt isn't on fire before handing it back to him.

"It's not like Casey and SS haven't seen you shirtless before. Like, every day at the pool."

Not-so-rabid-wolf tears his shirt out of my hands, turns his back to us, and puts it back on.

Another machine falls through the floor.

Annoying Niggle is back and reminding me that it's not

a great sign that we don't hear the machines thud on another floor below.

I remind Annoying Niggle that the floor below might be soft enough that the machines hit without a sound.

But the other possibility unnerves me. That there *isn't* any floor below.

But then, wouldn't we hear the whooshing sound that we heard when Franc joined us? The sound of air leaving the ship? And wouldn't we feel like we're out of air?

Out of air. I turn back to the wall bubble. I pound on it. "Let them out!" I yell.

I hear one muffled voice in response. It sounded like, "Hello?"

Water advances across the ceiling.

Now we're all pounding on the bubble's wall.

More machines fall through. More wires streak across the floor. We push ourselves into the furthest corner of the room, on one side of Crumbles, Billy, and Jared's prison.

"Can you hear me? Push your hand into a wall hole," I yell. Which probably makes more sense to us and to you than it does to them.

We hear a muffled, "Hello?" back. They can't make out my words.

A drop of water drips on my face. Pop. A big box falls through. Pop. Another slides into a hole.

"The boys can fall sideways!" Not-so-rabid wolf sometimes says stuff nobody understands. Don't feel bad, it's not just you.

Tim runs to the air-conditioning-like box and yanks on the empty metal tube that runs out of it.

"Help me."

Casey runs over and wrestles with the tube as well. I

still don't know what we're doing, but I'm happy to go along with Tim's idea.

Yeah, I know. After talking all morning about how he's the king of bad ideas, I'm now aiding and abetting him.

But you aren't on the spaceship with us, about to hear your cat suffocate to death, or watch your friend and brother fall into outer space, to certain death.

In this scenario, you'd listen to someone with a history of crazy ideas, too. Crazy is just what we need right now.

Sarah and I join in, and all four of us pull the metal tubing free.

Standing next to the white bubble, where the room is still relatively dry, Tim rips the metal tubing in half and holds it length-wise so the end sticks out into the middle of the room. You know, where it's legitimately raining.

The water slides down the tube and pools at Tim's feet.

"What are you doing?" I reach out to snatch the tube from him, but he steps to the side and angles the tube so it runs water over the bubble wall.

It's a dangerous game he's playing. The water runs down the bubble wall and puddles at our feet. But the bubble wall starts to turn blue.

We huddle where the bubble wall and the room's wall meet. I wish I could turn to look at the door we came in to see if we could get back to it without falling through the floor, but my gaze is glued on Tim's feet.

I watch to make sure he's not about to tumble through. As if looking really hard at his feet will keep him here with us.

Ridiculous, I know.

The pool of water on the floor creeps toward my brother's florescent green sneakers, and I can't wait any longer. I thrust my hand into the bubble wall. It goes all the way through. I wave it around like a maniac until someone grabs it.

I feel shivers up my spine. Holding Billy's hand. Electrifying, like I always imagined.

I yank as hard as I can and fall backwards. He tumbles out with me, onto me.

Now, don't get all excited, it's not as thrilling as it sounds. We're a mess of flailing body parts since I've also fallen onto Sarah.

And then I pick up my head and get ready for this super romantic moment with the guy I just saved (well, Tim saved him too—credit) and look directly into the big brown eyes of ....

Jared. My nemesis.

CHAPTER 18

BACK IN THE DISSOLVING SAFETY OF THE EVAPORATING CORRIDOR

It's not as if I puckered up for a kiss or anything, but I'm embarrassed I thought holding Jared's hand was all electrifying. I still have saving to do—of the right boy—so I stand up, dust off and realize that Billy is standing over me, glowering.

Weird.

Did I do something wrong?

He must have followed Jared out through the hole in the wall.

Tim has the peace of mind to catch Crumbles as she jumps through the hole. Our cat is a bundle of hisses and claws, so I reach out to pet her head.

There's no time to explain the whole we're-on-a-space-ship thing. Not if we don't want to fall through the floor into whatever is or isn't below us.

Sarah grabs Jared's hand, I grab Billy's (!!) and we side-step along the wall until we reach the door spot.

Tim finds it quickly and sticks his hand through, opens it, and we all tumble out the other side.

The golden glow of the walls is a relief after the stark whiteness of the inner room. It's also a relief that the lights are back on, and that the Clanker is nowhere in sight.

Maybe things are looking up.

I feel all around the corridor floor with my hands.

Dry as dust.

My whole body relaxes, and I feel muscles I didn't even know I had. I guess I've been holding my body pretty rigid during the whole it's-raining-inside-and-that-makes-stuff-fall-through-the-floor/two-boys-are-trapped-and-may-not-have-enough-air-in-a-weird-wall-bubble-thing.

And I'm kind-of expecting some gratitude.

Not of the kowtow and kiss my feet variety.

But you know, thanks is a pretty strong word.

Instead:

"What the hell, Kells?" Billy stands above me (again) with his hands on his hips.

I've never seen him mad before. He must be pretty disoriented.

"Hey." Sarah plants two hands on Billy's chest and pushes him back.

If there's anything Sarah hates, it's rudeness. Oh, and rudeness toward her best friend?

The worst.

If you think Sarah is a meek, shy girl, you have no idea how quickly she can turn into ... well, a rabid wolf.

Plus, I don't think people get to use a nickname when they're mad. And mad for no good reason too.

Does he think I am responsible for him being on a spaceship? Well, Annoying Niggles has been hinting at that very thing for a little while.

I just don't have time to pay attention.

Now weirdly, Tim AND Jared both start shoving poor Billy. Does everyone on this spaceship have a thing about rudeness?

I try not to even see Jared, because I know that looking at him will just bring the Incident back to me.

And I can't lose it any more than I already have on this spaceship. I need all my wits about me.

I know what you are thinking. But Billy just isn't showing his best colors right now. He really *is* boyfriend material. But he's been in a tiny box with a jerk of a guy for too long and suddenly being on a spaceship can be scary.

I should know.

And sometimes when boys—well, anyone—get scared, they get angry.

I've seen it with my brother, the now-not-so-rabid wolf all the time. It's not his fault, just like it's not Billy's fault right now.

But it is unfortunate, because it would be kind-of cool to be on a space adventure with not-scared Billy.

Electrifying, in fact.

"Stop it, everyone." I stand up and walk down the corridor past the door we just left. Over my shoulder I bring everyone up to speed.

"We're on a spaceship, the walls and floors disintegrate when they get wet, and we need to figure out how to get back to Earth. The control room is one floor above us, but the ship's controls electrocute anyone who tries to use them. And we don't have … stairs."

Because I haven't seen any means of going up or down on this spaceship at all.

I don't even turn around to see if people follow me. I know Sarah, Tim, and Casey will.

I could care less about whatever Jared decides to do at this point—he pretty much makes it his business to always disagree with me.

And it's not like I can control Billy. I am starting to be thrilled that the Coke fortune is coming true, though.

Who knew that could happen? In space?

Casey's voice follows me and explains what he discovered in the machine room.

"So, the big cable did come through the ceiling, and right into the cell that the guys were trapped in. So that's what led from the control center. It wasn't a parallel circuit, just a big one."

"That means that there isn't a parallel control panel, right?" Good, Tim is following me too. "NO, CRUMBLES!" I hear a struggle, some yelps of pain from Tim, and then Crumbles' furry form streaking past me and around the next corner of the corridor.

Great. Our cat is on the loose.

I hope Billy snaps out of whatever funk he's in soon, but that's his problem, really, not mine.

My problems are starting to number more than I can count, like the number of maraschino cherries my brother would put on a sundae if I let him.

I mean, I'm leading a group of mainly rabid wolves through a dissolving spaceship with no understanding of how it works, and praying to the Coke gods that we don't come across the Clanker.

Maybe I should get serious about taking control and driving this thing back to Earth.

(As if I've just been fooling around this whole time.)

CHAPTER 19

EARTHLING ISSUES CREATE A PILE-UP

"I think we're going the wrong way." Jared's annoying voice follows me down the space corridor. Of course, he's disagreeing with me—that's been his MO since kindergarten.

You might be wondering how a perfectly normal and well-adjusted girl like me gets a nemesis. I'm aware, not all girls have a nemesis, but let me reassure you, it is a perfectly natural thing.

Especially once you understand the circumstances of how it all happened.

Nemesis might be too light of a description, but humor makes everything easier to handle.

A lesser gracious girl than me might have become Jared's nemesis years ago, when he started calling me Katie (totally NOT my name) and just because his default position is to do the opposite of whatever I say.

Some defaults are healthy coping mechanisms—like how I ignore not-so-rabid wolf, Tim. Some defaults are just annoying. But lots of people are annoying, and all those people aren't my nemeses.

Just one. Because of the Incident.

Speaking of ignoring—Tim is yanking so hard on my sleeve that I think he's going to rip it off.

"What?!" I don't mean to yell, but I think I'm still unnerved that Billy seems so angry.

"Don't you hear it?" Tim shakes his head and his whole body.

I stop walking and cock my head to listen. Yes, people do that. Not because it makes me hear better, but because then the not-so-rabid wolf knows I'm doing what he wants me to do. It's no skin off my nose to throw him a bone every once in a while.

But then I do hear it.

Sarah and I exchange a sinking look.

Clanking. Coming toward us, from the direction we're facing.

About face!

I pull Tim back toward the door we just exited.

Not for the first time, I wonder how anything makes that much metallic noise on the soft, pillowy floor.

"Back so soon? Decide I was right after all, Katie?" Jared's voice is always calm, which belies the hidden malice.

I ignore Jared. Even though he's not my brother, he definitely falls into the rabid wolf category.

Luckily the corridor stems off in both directions from the control room, so if we keep walking, we'll get ... somewhere, at least underneath the control room, right? Not for the first time today, I wish I had schematics for this spaceship.

I explain the noise to our newest astronauts. "Do you guys hear that? There is something here, and it's coming toward us, something clanking. A Clanker. We need to get away."

I want to run, but I also don't want to scare Tim and Casey.

Billy catches my hand. "Okay." He smiles. There's the Billy I know and would like to date.

We start walking. All of us.

I'm trying not to think of our cat running into the Clanker.

"How do you know that it's something bad? How do you know we should walk away from it?" Yup, Jared misses no opportunity to disagree with me.

I take a deep breath. I know how to be calm in the face of Rabid Nemeses. "What's the worst thing that can happen?" I turn to face Jared.

He looks confused. He's no longer smiling and a crease has appeared on his forehead.

"What do you mean?"

"I mean, we are trapped on a spaceship. In space." It is always a good idea to repeat important concepts to Rabid Nemeses. "The worst thing that a clanging noise can be is something bad that wants to ..." I look at Tim's eyes, and think hard about how I'm going to say this in front of my little brother. "... keep us from getting back home."

I'm not sure my brother has ever really grasped the direness of our situation. I'm planning on keeping it that way.

Jared looks at Tim and Casey and back to me. "You're right." He says. "Let's go." He walks off.

I'm WHAT?

I'm right?!

Jared has never uttered those words in the history of our nemeses.

And now he has the audacity to start leading us all, like it is his idea in the first place?

As if he's been on this spaceship the whole time?

I might not know much about the ins and outs of this ship, but I've been to a few more rooms than he has. I've been to the most important room. I'd like to get back to the control room, in fact. I look above us to where I imagine the control room to be. How can we get back up?

If only there had been a way to leave Jared in that little bubble and just save Billy.

Who, if you happen to notice, is still holding my hand.

Sarah notices, and gives me a crooked grin. Like she's saying, 'he's cute, I know you have liked him for a while, but he was rude a few minutes ago. Be careful.' Not that SS holds a grudge, she doesn't. But she's so loyal to me, she won't let the rudeness pass. Not until he fixes it.

The only reason I follow Jared down the hallway is because I can't get in front of him while holding Billy's hand. It would be kinda awkward to rush Billy in front of Jared and might make it seem as though I care more about winning over Jared than showing Billy that I like him.

Don't worry, I have my priorities in order.

I sweetly shove Sarah in front of us, so she can follow our bouncing brothers' heads down the corridor. That way I can make sure that everyone is safe.

Bringing up the rear is actually an important spot to be in. And I can yell at Jared if he leads us somewhere wrong. Believe me, I'm happy to. He deserves a lot more than getting yelled at.

"All I was thinking about in that white cell was you." Billy's voice is all silky in the spaceship. Like the acoustics are perfect for a suave-and-cool-asking-out conversation.

I try to arrange my facial features to be all open and

relaxed, but I just can't forget that we're trapped on a spaceship and that my brother's and everyone's lives are in danger.

If Billy wants to ask me out here, it'll be memorable for sure!

A tingle of electricity shoots up my arm and down into my stomach, where there seems to be an electrical storm raging around the last morsels of my digesting grilled cheese. I ignore Annoying Niggle which asks why anyone would be thinking of dating while trapped in a padded bubble.

Jared turns around just to stare at Billy.

Billy stares back.

It's none of my nemesis's business what is happening between us. "Just lead, if you want to be in front so much!" I should just ignore him, but I don't.

The clanking noises grow louder. Closer.

I wave Jared forward with my free hand. Why does everything seem to be in slow motion? Jared starts walking again, jogging really, and we follow. But the clanking picks up the pace too.

Billy seems not to care about the Clanker. "So ... you have pretty eyes. And you're super kind."

I'm not sure why this annoys me SO MUCH. He seems to not understand at all, the seriousness of our situation.

Don't get me wrong. If we were back on Earth, and Billy rode by my house and happened to stop and get off his bike and we got a chance to sit in the crook of the tree behind my house and Sarah kept the brothers happy inside, probably by letting them take apart someone's old VCR or something and Billy took my hand and said all these slow and kind and sweet things to me, it would melt my heart.

But right now, the boy better get to the point.

Not that I want him to ask me out in front of my brother.

But this your-eyes-are-pretty stuff feels like a kind of slow-dripping-water-torture kind of thing.

Ever since we fell into this spaceship, I've felt like there is a ticking clock counting down. Counting down to when we get too far from home to get back. Counting down to when the oxygen runs out. Counting down to when the whole interior of the ship gets wet and we fall out into space. Counting down to when that Clanker finds us.

I don't have time to tiptoe around the issue.

And I know something about counting down. I read somewhere that if people think in terms of days instead of months, then time seems shorter. The article was all about how to get more school work done—students will work harder if they have thirty days rather than one month before a project is due.

I know it's all in my head, but I'll use any trick to get through the year! And so, since the Incident, I've been counting down time in the smallest amounts possible. For instance, there's only six hundred sixty nine thousand, six hundred seconds of school left in the year.

Even I can survive that. The right kind of countdown is extremely useful. And easy. I have an app on my phone.

"So, you want to go out with me?" I ask Billy. I don't have time to wait for a boy to ask me out. I only have seconds left in the school year.

See how that works?

I don't turn to look at him, although I'd kill to see the expression on his face. He pauses mid stride, and I pull him forward, back into a jog.

But Jared stops short in front of us. Tim stops as well, but Casey isn't paying attention and bumps into Jared.

Sarah reaches forward to keep Casey from falling, but forgets that the walls are soft and loses her balance when she tries to brace herself on the wall.

I'm in the middle of yanking Billy back into movement. This is a really long way to say that before I get an answer from Billy, we all fall into a piled mess on the floor.

Jared untangles himself first, which isn't all that fair, since he was the cause of the pile-up. "Don't you want to think about it, Kelly?"

But he's not looking at me, he's looking angrily at Billy.

Billy pulls himself up and steps back.

The clanking sounds really loud now.

Sarah gets up too, and I'm surprised that she is the one who pulls me to my feet.

Didn't I just get a boyfriend? I might be new at the boyfriend-girlfriend stuff, but shouldn't my boyfriend help me to my feet?

But he's too busy shaking his head at Jared. Like they have some stupid boy-bond. And I know they aren't friends and certainly aren't best friends like SS and me. So, I'm further annoyed that they are acting that way.

Shouldn't my first boyfriend moment be sealed with a kiss?

The clanking, super close now—right beyond where we can see behind us down the sloping hallway—startles that thought right out of my head.

"Let's go!" I push my way past Jared.

I trail my hand along the golden wall and hope to find a door that we can escape through before the Clanker reaches us.

CHAPTER 20

LITERALLY RUNNING IN OBLONGS

So, if we weren't being chased by some unknown but loud clanking something, I'd stop to tell you about the Incident. You know, the thing that made Jared and I nemeses.

I know I said I wouldn't tell you about it, but now that Jared is here, I feel like you have a right to know. Otherwise, you might think that I'm treating him meanly.

Once you know, you'll realize that I am being more kind than he deserves.

And, okay, since I'm just running down the hallway, pushing into the wall with my hand looking for a reverse doorknob and trying not to think about how I just asked a guy—THE GUY—out and how he hasn't actually told me yes or no, but who am I kidding, I'm sure he'll say yes, or at least, he would have already said yes if it weren't for the Incident, I'll tell you a little bit.

It all started nineteen million, four hundred forty thousand one hundred seconds ago at lunch in the Hillside Middle School cafeteria.

I'm sure that doesn't surprise you. A lot of the worst *and* best stuff happens in or near a middle school cafeteria.

Like the awesome time we all had a food fight UNDER the tables so the teachers didn't even know it was going on until we left and the floor beneath the tables were covered in disgusting spaghetti, blue Gatorade, and mashed potatoes. (A remarkably purple mess.)

Or the time I found out that some shmuck named Adam was picking on SS and I totally defended her and put him in his place. But this wasn't one of those times—this was a worst time.

Anyway, I don't know if you've figured it out by now, but I'm not one of those girls who doesn't eat like a normal human being. (Now I'm sounding like Franc.)

I like my grilled cheese, I like my Coke, and sometimes in the cafeteria, I like my club sandwich with extra mayo and french fries.

My point being that on the day in question, I had a full plate of food in front of me, and I was focused.

On the food.

My stomach grumbles—it has been way too long since that breakfast grilled cheese—and I stick my hand into the wall as if a doorknob, or whatever the opposite of doorknob is, maybe knob hole, will appear just because I want it to.

Knob-hole sounds like a bad word.

The clanking echoes behind us. Sometimes I catch something metal out of the corner of my eyes. And I'm starting to realize that we're really going around and around in a circle. Or, rather, an oblong.

Maybe you already realized the physics of the spaceship. But I've been busy keeping the not-so-rabid wolves alive.

My stomach grumbles again. I'm not starving. But my stomach isn't happy.

"Hey Kells." Billy says.

I'm also not one of those girls who thinks she's ugly when she's not. I mean, I'm not model pretty, or Amy Pond pretty, but I'm totally cute. Like I said before, girl-next-door cute. I'm not stuck up about it, but I know I'm date-worthy. Not that pretty is the only requirement for being date-worthy.

I have plenty of friends who aren't traditionally cute, but are awesome and some of them have totally devoted boyfriends or girlfriends. The others really should, but teenage boys (and girls) aren't the most evolved.

Anyway, my parents call me "a catch." They've been saying that with more regularity since the Incident. As if to reassure me. I don't know about what—maybe that middle school will sometime end?

They also call Tim "energetic."

You can draw your own conclusions.

So, it's not that I'm worried about the next words that are going to come out of Billy Fowler's mouth, but you know, I'm not *not* worried.

"Hey." I've picked up the pace again, and I'm almost running. Which might be why we're talking in such few words.

The lights above us are stark white now and worse than the florescent lights in the changing room at the Macys in the mall. It's not romantic at all.

"So, you, um …." His words drift off.

Not romantic at all.

"Yes. I asked you out." Like I said, I know I'm a catch.

I'm trying not to think about the Incident. Like if I don't think about it, he'll totally forget about it.

Because that's how minds work.

"Yes. You did." He huffs. I guess that swimming (my sport) is better cardiovascular practice than basketball (his) for running through a soft-floored spaceship.

"So ...." I'm not patient. And I need to focus on us not getting caught by the thing behind us.

"So ...."

Omg. Boys are so impossible. Remember? Crazy.

"So ...."

I would take Franc back in a second if I have to listen to Billy Fowler flounder much more.

I try to remember how hard my heart pounds every time he bikes past our house. Is it a sign that my heart is only pounding because we're running?

Pounding heart—good. A spaceship ruining what should be one of the best moments of my awful middle school career—tragic.

"So. Yes." Billy finally gets to the point.

My hand pushes through a part of the wall so fast that I get stuck up to my elbow, while my feet continue to run past. My arm wrenches, and I jerk back and fall to the side.

A door! I found a door.

I pick myself up, open the door, and hustle everyone through.

"Did you and Billy just decide to date?" Jared weirdly stops to help me untangle my arm from the door.

"Yes. Why should you care?" I pull free. Of the door.

"I don't. I mean. I do. You shouldn't date him." He shrugs his shoulders which is about the most generic thing anyone can do.

As if. As if the person responsible for the Incident gets ANY SAY in my love life.

Sarah gives me a *look* as she ushers our brothers through the open space.

I push Jared—hard—through the doorway.

I hop into the room and slam the door.

But not before I see a towering mechanical robot-type thing round the corner. And I don't really understand what I'm seeing because I swear that I see two creatures, one walking—bouncing really—on top of another.

But now I'm safely on the other side of the soft door. I listen for clanking but can't hear any.

Maybe because not-so-rabid wolf is saying my name every half second and poking me in the arm.

My arm has a permanent bruise in one specific spot from his poking. At the very least I can say that he is laser-pointer accurate.

I don't even get to celebrate my new girlfriend status for a second.

Or yell at Jared, finally, for the Incident.

Because we are all standing on a ledge about a foot and a half wide. The floor in front of us literally melts down into the room below.

It's hard to tell, but we seem to be standing on the opposite side of the machine room we were in before, the room we just left. And the room is still melting.

Most of the machines lie cock-eyed an entire floor below us, on top of what looks thick, white, marshmallow frosting (melted floor, I guess), and that's on top of what-ever used to be in the room below. Beneath all the layers, sit some weird butt-pinching white marshmallow couches and chairs.

As if this room used to be someone's huge living room.

In space.

Our situation has not improved. Out of the frying pan and into the marshmallow-melted mess. One story below.

"Like I said, You shouldn't date him. You deserve better." Jared leans against the wall like he's hanging out at the Geoff's, talking about whatever boys like to talk about over pizza and a Coke.

"I'm standing right here, man." Billy is on the other side of Jared, unfortunately. I can't get in between them if they start fighting again.

Jared turns to look Billy square in the eyes. "Then you know exactly what I'm talking about. She deserves better." He looks around at the mess. "Lightyears better."

Look at that, Jared getting in on the space theme. It took him long enough.

Billy and Jared exchange a look. I don't have time to wonder what that look means.

Because the ledge is getting smaller and the tiny patch of floor I'm standing on is slippery.

The floor is wet.

"Back out before we fall!" I pop the door open a crack and see the mechanical two-creature stationed outside.

I close the door.

And whisper.

"We can't go that way. We're trapped."

CHAPTER 21

CHUCKS: SLIPPERY WHEN WET

So, yeah, around nineteen million, four hundred forty thousand one hundred seconds ago (give or take 100 seconds or so—I'm not pulling my phone out right now to check, and the app probably doesn't work in space, anyway) I was in the Hillside Middle School cafeteria getting ready to tuck into some serious lunch-time chowing when Sarah came running up (gracefully as always) but looking as pale as my weirdly white french fries.

What kind of potato makes a completely white fry?

Or more to the point, what kind of fryer leaves a fried french fry white?

"Kelly, I'm so sorry!" Of course, I don't remember right now exactly what she said. But Sarah apologizing for something that's not her fault is something she does.

However, I do remember.

Every. Single. Moment.

Of what happened next.

BUT IN THE universe's scheme of things, that moment doesn't have anything on this one.

I literally have all my eggs in this one Easter-egg-spaceship basket.

My brother. My best friend. Her brother. And the guy I like-like and the guy I hate.

And it feels like some of the eggs are going to crack.

Or maybe my sanity is. Or already did.

That's the only reason I can think of why I would be obsessing over a bully like Jared when I just asked out Billy-grilled-cheese-Fowler, and HE SAID YES.

He said yes!

My feet slide forward until my toes dangle out over a solid one-story fall to the room below.

Well, not solid. Nothing is solid on this melting, Easter egg spaceship.

Nothing.

Tim grabs my arm. He looped around Jared to get to me when he noticed I was sliding. That kid notices everything! But my Chucks have less traction than his sneakers, and it's clear that I either have to go back through the door and face the robot double-decker alien or fall down to the room below.

I don't like either choice.

And if I fall, I'll probably take my brother with me.

No way I'm pulling Tim into a big fall.

Tim won't let go, and I don't want to pull away from him to turn toward the door—then we both *will* go over.

He shoves my arm back through the door's knob hole.

I feel around within the door for anything to grab onto, but it's kind-of like what you would imagine grabbing onto the stay-puff marshmallow man would be like.

All soft and gushy.

I slide a little and pull on the door to stop me.

It opens a crack, inward instead of outward.

I slam it shut. As much as you can slam a soft door into a soft wall.

I can't chance that the mechanical two-monster is out there waiting for us.

I have to stop pulling on the door.

Leaning into the wall helps a little. It feels like I'm pushing into a slightly-under-baked pizza crust. I'm not falling, yet.

I turn around and push my regular-sized-thank-you-very-much butt into the wall.

"Lean back." I'm normally better at sounding calm when I'm under stress, but my voice is shrill and hurts even my own ears.

"Can we make it to a wider part of the floor?" Sarah points to where a few machines still stand on this level, like on a shelf.

"Let's try." I motion Tim to move in that direction, and he literally dances past Jared, Billy, Sarah, and Casey to lead the way. That kid has moves.

We form the thinnest possible straight line—little boys in the front—Sarah next with a hand on Casey, then Billy makes Jared go around him so he can keep me on the ledge, and we start to tightrope-walk toward the peninsula of floor.

Well, tightrope-walk like we have inner-ear balance issues. We're all leaning so far into the wall that we look all crooked. Like hunchbacks of Notre Dame, only we're hunching to the side. And leaning while walking isn't doing much to keep my feet from sliding out from under me.

Tim glances back every few feet to make sure we're all still on the ledge.

Bang-crash-slurp.

A refrigerator sized-machine falls through the floor and hits another machine on its way down.

It settles into the graveyard of alien machines.

That's going to be me in a moment. Less than a moment.

My feet slip and Billy—my NEW BOYFRIEND—grabs my shirt. For a moment, one of my feet is dangling out into space (room space, not outer space, and I take a moment to be grateful for that).

See, it totally could be worse.

But not much, because while the grip that Billy has on my shirt is awesomely strong, the grip that my shirt has on my pants is not.

Sarah hears me gasp, turns around, notices that my shirt is lifting off my torso, and scoots back past Jared to clamp her hands onto my shirt, right around my chest.

So, yeah. My belly is hanging out, but at least my breasts and bra aren't.

Yet.

You'd think that the horror of hanging off a ledge would be worse than the horror of two boys from your middle school seeing your breasts, but you'd be completely wrong.

Completely.

There are things that are worse than falling to one's death. Lots, in fact.

Between Sarah's and Billy's grasps, I manage to settle myself as securely as I can back on the ledge.

I'm pretty sure that the heat from my face is further melting the floor.

I smooth my shirt back over my gut and try to ignore my embarrassment. I'm not dead, I tell myself. For some reason that doesn't seem to matter as much as it should.

What if Billy decides not to date me because I'm clumsy, or because he wasn't ready to see my pale, not-so-firm stomach?

We all start inching along again.

Don't get me wrong, I'm not completely self-conscious, but *you* flash (or almost flash) your prospective boyfriend, and let *me* know how that feels.

You know, after months and months of people at school treating you like you have the Cheese-Touch.

"Got you." Billy says. Phew, he still sounds like he cares for me. He puts a hand on Jared, making him wait and pushes me gently past him so I can walk between him and Sarah. Sarah offers me her hand, but if I do fall, I don't want to pull her down.

Instead I focus on shuffling and keeping my momentum going forward and not off the side. I try to stare only at my feet and not look down at the long drop.

I hear a noise from Jared behind Billy, kind of like Jared is strangling a cat or something.

Where's Crumbles? Did she get past the double-decker alien? Is she safe?

I know I'm trying to distract myself from what just happened, twelve seconds ago.

But I'm also concerned for my cat. I feel guilty that I didn't mention her in the all-my-eggs-are-aboard-this-basket list.

I walk softly forward, lost in my thoughts about my cat, and realize that Sarah is way ahead of me, helping her brother and Tim onto the larger patch of floor ahead.

And Billy and Jared are fighting in low tones behind me. Fighting like it might erupt into a fist fight any second.

Crazy, rabid-wolf boys.

Nobody is close to me, and my feet start to slip.

By now you probably realize the same thing that I've realized.

That it's a pretty decent idea to wear sensible shoes with excellent traction on an every-day basis. Everyone else is wearing sneakers.

Not that my Chucks are five-inch heels or anything. But, boy, are they slippery. Especially when wet. There's close to no treads at all anymore on the bottom.

So, shoot me for wanting to look cute on the off chance that Coke fortune came true. Which, of course, it did come true. And now I have a boyfriend, maybe? Plus, I love my Chucks.

But when I get home, I'm totally wearing sneakers twenty-four-seven.

Maybe even to bed.

Just in case I find myself falling into an alien space craft.

There is no way for me not to fall—I've passed the point of no return on this slip. There's no best friend or brother to grab at me, there's no new boyfriend to save me by the skin of my shirt.

I'm falling.

Tim's voice rings out. "Jump, K, JUMP!"

CHAPTER 22

NOT ONE MORAL LEG TO FALL ONTO

I remember that moment, nineteen million, four hundred forty thousand three hundred forty seconds ago, when I saw that pained look on Sarah's face and I felt like I was falling just like I'm falling now.

At Hillside Middle School cafeteria, it took me a few minutes to get her to talk—and in those moments I thought maybe someone had died.

And I was really concerned, because our brothers were visiting the middle school that day—step-up day—and you know what kind of havoc my brother can reap.

Maybe Time had put a mechanical pencil into a pencil sharpener, or had released the pet mice in the biology classroom, or had inadvertently caused someone's death. Maybe his own.

But it turned out that nobody was dead, except my reputation.

Sarah managed to push the words "Boy's bathroom" out of her lips.

I still thought something terrible had happened to one

of our brothers—rabid-wolves in my school had preoccupied me all day.

So, of course I had to go see. "Is it Tim? Casey? Sarah, what's wrong?!"

But she just shook her head back and forth and refused to talk at all.

What could I do, except head to the nearest boy's bathroom.

I heard her yelling after me, "NO, Kelly, no!"

I turned, and she was running toward me. I was a little confused, because Sarah had come to get *me*, and now she didn't want see whatever was making her act like someone died? Sometimes best friends get caught between should-do and would-like-to-do.

I can't blame her. In hindsight, this one thing might have been better if I didn't see it. But as a best friend, you can't make that call for your friend.

There are two boy's bathrooms near the cafeteria, and I headed to the closer one.

Right now, though, I'm headed straight for the floor.

Luckily, I hear my brother and react (I'm well trained to act quickly where he is concerned).

Instead of just sliding off the edge, at the last nanosecond, I jump.

My free-fall only lasts a fraction of a second, probably. But I have plenty of time to think about that day in the cafeteria *and* how I might get creamed like creamed corn at Thanksgiving when I land *and* what a very bad idea this is.

But, instead of falling into the jagged edge of an upturned metal box directly below the ledge, I'm now aiming for a couch-type thing that looks like it's made of the same material as the walls and floors, lying haphazardly across an upturned metal box.

I'm hoping it's as marshmallow-soft as it looks.

I hit hard, but the couch gives.

I wish I could tell you that I spin off it in a great ninja move, but I don't. I bang off the couch into a machine and then flip back into the couch.

Upside-down.

Regular-sized butt straight up in the air. My only consolation is that I am wearing sensible (cute!) shorts and not a skirt. Certain girl attire is just no good on an alien space ship.

"Geronimo!" Tim yells as he jumps off the ledge.

He doesn't give me time to sharply bark, 'no.' I don't even have any time to rub my bruises.

All I can do is dive out of the way.

Sarah sensibly lowers her brother down until he is closer to the floor, drops him, and then she lowers herself by holding onto the ledge with both hands, swings out, and lets go. Holy Taco Tuesday, she's graceful even mid-fall.

"Thanks, Tim." Because his yell kept me from falling from the floor above and cracking my head on the machine guts around us.

Credit.

My New Boyfriend and the Knob-hole Jared follow our lead and jump safely down.

One is slightly more coordinated than the other; I won't tell you which one. You might start to like the wrong one.

"You okay?" The wrong one asks me that.

I just glare at him.

A part of my brain is still in the past—in that moment

in the middle school bathroom, and I know I'm supposed to be all forgive-and-let-live, but I'm not that evolved.

My New Boyfriend echoes the sentiment. "Are you okay?"

I smile as I get up, even though everything seems to hurt, especially the back of one knee (oddly enough) because I don't need to be all damsel-in-distress.

I'm going to get us off this spaceship, which means I'm the one in charge. "I'm fine."

Casey is already inspecting all the machines that are in various stages of totally demolished to actively sparking to just fine.

Tim is inspecting with him, by running his hands over everything.

I roll my eyes. I should tell him to stop.

What did sparks get us earlier in the day?

I'd be happy if you'd forget the part I played with the hose, but even I can't forget that part, since that water is still making us fall through stuff.

I kneel down and feel around, but the floor seems completely dry. For now. Stupid me with the hose.

"So, are we boyfriend and girlfriend? That really happened, right?" Billy throws himself onto the couch and lounges there, motioning me over with his hand.

Which is really cute. And totally boyfriend-like.

I could definitely see us watching Armageddon in our third-floor movie room back home. But since right now, we're pretty much living Armageddon (except as far as I know, the Earth isn't going to explode), I don't really have time to sit.

But I also don't want to offend him 365 seconds after we started going out.

I ignore Jared, who does seem to want to offend My

New Boyfriend with a great big snort. It's annoying when people exaggerate for attention.

I watch my brother out of one eye and cross the marshmallowy floor to the couch and My New Boyfriend. "That happened."

I spin in a circle, taking in the whole room. I want to make sure there aren't any puddles in the floor—who knows what might or might not be below us. We can't afford to fall through another level.

I touch his shoulder, hoping it conveys the message of we're-definitely-boyfriend-and-girlfriend-and-I'd-super-like-to-stop-and-make-out-but-my-brother-and-my-nemesis-are-in-the-room-and-we're-in-danger-of-falling-out-into-space.

Sarah hovers over our brothers, which lets me walk the perimeter to make sure that there aren't any gushy floor parts.

Casey's voice rings out from across the room.

The pillow walls and floors are great for acoustics. Maybe this Easter egg ship belongs to alien musicians.

"Hey. It was a parallel processing cable, after all! Here's the duplicate control panel, Kelly. Just what we were looking for, right?!"

I think about Sarah's alarm clock in pieces in her room. Sarah was just glad that Casey had put her phone back together before he took apart the alarm clock. She never gets mad that he takes things apart since everything's always better after he makes adjustments and puts them back together.

I walk over to what Casey, Tim, and now Sarah are inspecting.

It's the great big refrigerator-sized machine with the TV

screen in it. The one that we could see My New Boyfriend and Knob Hole arguing in before.

On the back is a panel hanging open like an open laptop, and it does look exactly like what was in front of me when I was trying to drive the space ship two floors up in the control room.

"Don't touch anything—it could electrocute you!"

Ignoring me, Casey puts his hands around the outer edges of the panel and move some dials. "Maybe I could figure it out. But I have to see the other one in the control room. And some of you have to stay here, to see if they are connected. See if this one changes when I change the one in the control room. This one could be completely broken."

My New Boyfriend comes up behind me and puts his hands on my shoulders. He leans in and kisses the back of my neck, which zaps me with nice electricity right into my grilled-cheese-less stomach. "Kid, I don't think messing with alien technology will get us home. Just let us grown-ups do our thing."

So, I don't agree with the condescending attitude New Boyfriend is using, but I do agree with that plan.

Sarah shoots him enough daggers for the both of us.

"Casey, I don't see how this machine could get us home. I couldn't even get the first control panel to work." I pause for effect. "And no way are we splitting up."

Tim does a little jump. If you could call a giant leap into the air a little jump.

If he ever set his mind to basketball, or any sport, actually, he'd break some records. "Casey's right. There are matching buttons like this on the control panel. It's possible they connect."

Casey nods. "I think we can assume they connect, at least ...." his voice trails off. "Kelly, is it possible that you were thinking about ...” He swept his hand to include a glowering Jared and a gleaming Billy. “... while you were touching the control panel?”

I think back to those moments in the chaos when my hands stuck to the panel. “I wondered if I had fed Crumbles, I thought about Billy riding his bike past our house” I pause to blush, “and I thought about my nemesis.” I glare at Jared.

“Wait, I’m your nemesis?” Knob Hole turns and looks at me with all kinds of questions in his eyes.

“That’s the way you guys got here. Telepathic teleportation.” Casey nods to my brother, who grins and nods back, and Sarah beams like Casey just won the Nobel Peace Prize.

“Of course you’re my nemesis. You’ve been a jerk to me my whole life.” It is astounding what boys don’t pick up on. How could Jared think he is anything other than my nemesis?

I don’t even want to bring up Jared’s role in the boy’s bathroom that sealed the nemesis deal.

“And you choose to date *this guy*?” Jared spits out the words ‘this guy’ like they mean ‘serial killer.’

“Casey. Can we reverse it?” Tim is still nodding at Casey, like they are both telepathic and teleporting thoughts back and forth between them.

I stop shaking my head about Jared being crazy AND clueless and try to catch up.

Casey and Tim are light years ahead of me—they don’t want me to drive us home; they want me to *transport* everyone home. Like I transported Jared and Billy and Crumbles here—while I was being electrocuted.

I’m about to restate my position of doubt, but New Boyfriend condescends again. “Little dudes, leave the saving to us. There’s nothing you could possibly know about this tech—it's alien. Just shut up and go play. Let us think."

What Billy says might be true, but he doesn't have to be mean. I shake off Billy's hands and turn to defend my brother and his friend.

Annoyingly, Jared opens his big mouth before I can. "Ease off, man. You don't have a moral leg to stand on."

Which doesn't make much sense to me. I mean, that phrase doesn't make sense to begin with. How could legs be moral? And if they could, Jared's legs certainly didn't ooze with morality.

The opposite, in fact.

Anger flares from my empty stomach to flush my cheeks. And oddly, the anger makes me want to scream, yes, but also cry.

My New Boyfriend shoves my nemesis in the shoulder. "Shut up."

The guys face off, and one thing becomes clear.

Sarah and I and our little brothers are smack dab in the middle of a Big Rabid Wolf Fight.

They aren't just fighting because they were smooshed unexpectedly in that marshmallow cell on this Easter egg spaceship. They are in the middle of a bigger fight, one that I have no idea about, and even further, I don't *want* to know about.

These boys are crazy, and I'm happy to be clueless about the cause of their insanity right now.

Also, I'm starting to catch up to Casey and Tim's solution and my role in it.

I'm not looking forward to being electrocuted again.

Maybe I shouldn't drive.

CHAPTER 23
BAD WOLF

Sarah caught up with me half a second before I pulled open the door to the boy's bathroom at school.

"I'm sorry," she said again.

Or gasped, really, since she was huffing and puffing from running down the hall.

I'm telling you, swimming is a great cardio workout. My heart was pounding, but from sheer panic, not exertion.

"Don't ... open ... that ... door ...." Huffs and puffs.

I could have pushed past her in a second, she was in such a state.

But I hesitated, because that's what you do for best friends. You give them the benefit of the doubt. You give them a second, even when you are concerned for your brother's very safety and what might be behind the dreaded (in more ways than one) boy's bathroom door.

And at that moment, I probably should have just walked away.

Because what I saw next only hurt me.

If I find a time machine on this alien spacecraft, I will go back in time and tell myself not to open that door.

But of course, I opened the bathroom door.

And I saw the guy (who is right now in a spaceship talking about morals) behave like a first-class bully.

AND ON THIS SPACESHIP, far from the school bathroom, that moral-legs comment seems to open the can of worms that the big rabid wolves have been dancing around ever since we let them out of their marshmallow-y prison.

There is some serious rabid wolf bad behavior happening.

Bad wolf.

Bad, bad wolves.

They are literally circling one-another and spitting words out.

Spitting words at each other, even words without S'es in them, which are darn hard to spit.

"I have plenty of moral feet!" Billy swats his well-defined arm at Jared, which quite honestly isn't lending to the I-have-moral-feet argument. It does, however, support my rabid wolf hypothesis.

Jared holds up both arms in defense and circles around. "No moral feet. And no moral tree-climbing skills."

Billy turns an unflattering shade of spaghetti sauce red and sputters out a bunch of words I can't even understand.

I have to admit, there is a lot I'm not understanding right now.

One of those things is why we aren't trying to get off this spaceship right now.

"What are moral feet?" Tim taps directly on my arm bruise. Caramel Candy Corn, that boy has accurate aim.

"No idea. Morals?" But that didn't make much sense,

since Billy is captain of the Middle School JV Basketball team, and that's not a role they give to morally challenged people—I assume.

The captain of our girls' swim team is the nicest girl I know. Totally respectful. Even if she stopped hanging out with me after the whole boy's bathroom Incident. I don't hold it against our captain, or the rest of the team. What else could they do?

Plus, Jared is the one here who has the most questionable morals.

Not just questionable morals—no morals. Or the opposite. Are terrible morals a thing?

Billy continues to yell things at Jared. I can't make out everything, because he is so inflamed that all his words blur together, but certain phrases like, "keep your stupid nose out of my business" and "nobody asked you to get involved" come through.

Jared circles and yells things back. Like, "bad behavior is everyone's business." And self-righteous nonsense like that.

It reminds me of when people say 'it's like watching a train wreck.' I've never seen a train crashing, but I imagine you'd be watching it for awhile, because most trains are pretty long (at least all the ones that cross in front of us whenever we are late to get to the other side of town are Cheesy-bread long) and would take a long time to finish wrecking.

So, I watch and try to piece together what the rabid wolves are yelling about.

I'm also feeling pretty self-righteous. Because if there is one person in the room who should be granted the bad form to yell at someone, it's me, at Jared Bilkens.

Because when I opened that door to the boy's bathroom

that day, after giving Sarah a chance to convince me not to, then deciding that I had to know, I discovered a group of boys huddling around a disgusting limerick about Kelly Tate (me).

A disgusting, raunchy, unbelievable limerick, written in black sharpie, right there on the wall next to the mirror at the first sink. And, who, do you ask, was holding the black sharpie?

Why, one rabid-mean-terrible-bully-wolf named Jared Bilkens.

That's the image I see in my head every time someone whispers in class or looks at me in the cafeteria or points at me on the bus.

Jared spit-out-chewing-gum-stuck-to-the-bottom-of-your-shoe Bilkens penning a limerick about me on the boy's bathroom tile wall.

A picture of the limerick went viral (of course), and I had to ignore almost everyone in my grade all year except for Sarah and the swim team girls.

And the swim team girls only really spoke to me when we were in the pool. Although, since the limerick had to do with swimming, kind-of, I totally don't blame them.

Nobody wanted to be associated with it. With me.

And yet, I'm not the one yelling at Jared. My New Boyfriend is. And now you know why I'm so excited to have any boyfriend at all, let alone the very fit Billy Fowler.

I've kept my head up high.

I've skipped dances.

Stayed home from parties.

Watched movie after movie at home with my little brother.

But these things are hard to ignore. And now you know why Jared will always be my nemesis. And why I'm standing back and letting someone finally defend my honor to him.

I thought the high road was to ignore the bad behavior.

Now I think standing up for myself is much better.

Only, it doesn't really seem like My New Boyfriend is standing up for me. It looks more like he's defending his *own* honor.

But that can't be right.

The rabid wolves continue to yell at each other.

I watch.

Sarah watches too.

Jared Spoiled Milk Bilkens is finally getting his comeuppance.

Nothing else matters.

I'm happy feeling self-righteous.

It's not until Sarah tugs at my sleeve that I remember that we're on a spaceship that might drop us into space, at any moment, with a Clanker aboard.

"Where are the boys?" Sarah drops my sleeve and motions around the room.

The last time I saw our brothers is when Tim tapped my arm. Which was almost a whole argument ago.

I'm not in panic mode, yet, as I scan the room. Because seriously, where could they have gone?

But panic mode sets in pretty quick.

It's clear.

My brother and Casey aren't anywhere in the room.

They're gone.

CHAPTER 24

EVERYONE IS CRAZY AND CLUELESS EXCEPT FOR ME

I walk around to make sure.

They have to be here somewhere.

They're not.

The machine graveyard is spookily bare of little brothers.

"Shut up, both of you!" Sarah yells.

The fact that *she* is the one yelling panics me almost as much as the boys being missing.

I walk around the room a second time, mostly looking at the floor.

I don't want to tell Sarah, but I'm looking for holes that they might have fallen through.

No holes.

Except one in the corner which isn't big enough for a puppy, let alone a wolf to fall through.

"What's wrong?" Billy stops arguing long enough to figure out that things are even worse.

Jared is walking around the room already, pulling open cabinets in machines.

Which is actually smart.

Maybe they are still here, but we can't see where. An in-bad-taste game of hide-and-go-seek. Like where we found Billy and Jared trapped before.

I run over to the side of the room with the refrigerator TV and follow the cord back to the marshmallow cell. Only, of course, it doesn't connect—when it fell, it must have disconnected from the wall and the cell. But it leads me in the right direction.

The marshmallow cell is down here with us, if a little drooping and melted.

The hole we pulled the guys out of is still there, although it's now the size of a small bread bowl, and the shape of a bread bowl, halfway eaten.

I stick my head in. There are dim lights on the inside, lining the top and bottom, some hanging down like sagging Christmas lights.

It's clear nobody is inside.

Because my brain is short-wiring or something, I take the cord and re-connect the cell to the machine.

In fact, I walk all around, plugging things into walls and other machines. When I get a cord near the wall, the wall sucks it in with a shlooping sound and then a final-sounding clack.

I don't really know what I'm doing, but I always try to make things neater when I feel out of control.

My room has been ready for a white glove inspection for the past nineteen million, four hundred forty thousand eight hundred seconds.

Except for the laundry basket of not-quite dirty clothes, Tim's race car, and Casey's laptop, of course.

"Hey, what is it?" Billy is still standing in the middle of the room, doing nothing.

"Geez, can't you see that Tim and Casey are missing?" Jared yells at Billy like he's getting the last word in.

"The little guys? Missing?" If I wasn't beside myself because my brother and his best friend are gone, I would be a little annoyed that Billy isn't helping and doesn't seem to know what my brother's name is.

What kind of New Boyfriend is he?

But, like I said, I'm too busy with the crisis.

But not too beside-myself that I'm not a little annoyed when Jared finds the first clue.

He's my nemesis. He's not supposed to be helpful.

"Look at this!" he calls out from the wall at the other side of the room.

I pause my weird connect-plugs-to-odd-alien-tech activity and walk over.

Even Billy comes to see.

Jared's looking directly at the wall itself.

There are indents there, like little built-in shelves, each one big enough to hold a regular six-inch sub sandwich. All the shelves are the same color of the wall and completely disappear from view when I take a step back.

Jared points upward.

There's little built-in shelves all the way up, past where the room above used to be and there is a hole in the ceiling two stories up.

A rabid wolf sized hole.

The built-in shelves are like stairs, like a ladder in the wall.

"They climbed up there." Before I can even caution him against it, Jared starts scrambling up the indented ladder.

As I watch him go, I'm not *really* wishing that he falls and hits the floor hard. Not really.

I see the limerick scrawled into the spaceship's wall. I know it's only in my mind, you know, brain misfiring.

You'd think in space, I'd be able to escape it.

Clearly, you'd be wrong.

How had I been so distracted by the big-rabid wolves arguing that I missed my brother and Casey climbing up and out of the room?

Well, it wasn't just that—I had been remembering that moment in the boys' bathroom.

That always distracts me from what's important.

Jared Soggy-Croissants Bilkens ruins my life again.

I promise myself to never let that happen another time.

I pretend-punch Billy on the shoulder. He didn't help at all, him and whatever was more important to fight about than getting off this spaceship.

"Hey, you can't believe everything that people tell you!" Billy's tall frame turns toward me. His arms are crossed, and he's too close and not in the I'm-going-to-plant-a-romantic-kiss-on-your-lips way.

Sarah edges in between us, and Jared stops climbing to look down at us. Just for a moment—then he continues upward.

I try to make things playful again (as if they ever were really playful on this spaceship—but somebody's got to ease the tension) by laughing it off.

But then something stops me. There's a lot that's not making sense in what Billy and Jared are saying to each other. "Wait, what would people have told me?"

Billy stops glaring at me and turns to glare up at Jared.

Jared stares down at us and then double-times the climbing down.

"Did you find them? Are they up there?" Sarah asks.

"Yes, they are up there, and Jared is keeping it a SECRET

from all of us. He's great at keeping secrets. If he's smart that is." Billy backs up to let Jared climb down the last little bit. But he's still really close—this time to Jared.

How did I never notice that Billy is kind-of a bully?

Just my luck.

To be stuck on a spaceship with two bullies.

And clearly, there is something else I don't know, and contrary to not-so-rabid wolf, I'm not used to being clueless.

If I wasn't focusing on the where-on-the-spaceship-is-my-little-brother I would sit these two rabid wolves down and make them tell me what is going on.

Even though Billy's acting like a jerk, I'm still so lucky that he wants to date me—it's going to finally end the effects of the limerick on. My social life. He's my ticket to the end of hell at school. And maybe someone has to be a jerk to be strong enough to weather the storm that lives around me socially. All because of Jared and his meanness and his stupid sharpie.

"They aren't up there—but there is a door open to a corridor two flights up. They climbed up there, into a small room, and evidently out a door and into the hallway. What's two flights up?" Jared asks.

"The control room." Sarah and I both say it, almost in unison. Best friends.

"Let's go!" I start to climb, but Jared puts his hand on my foot.

"They wanted someone here to see if they could get that machine working. To try to send us all home."

I kick out at my nemesis.

Literally.

As if he can stop me from doing what I know I need to do. I need to go find my brother and keep him safe. "Yes. I know. Sarah and I will follow them and help them. You guys stay here and babysit the machines."

Perfect plan.

But Sarah shakes her head no. Her disagreeing is weird and makes me pause. She whispers to me, "Do we want to leave these two alone? I'm not sure both of them will be alive when we get back."

Which is a little tempting, depending on who's left. I'm pretty sure My New Boyfriend can hold his own against my String Cheese Nemesis.

But it won't get us home, if two rabid wolves are arguing instead of getting the job (whatever that might be) done.

"Okay, Sarah, you and Jared follow the boys. I'll stay here with Billy."

That way I'll have time to get back on the right page with my New Boyfriend.

Not that I'll be able to focus on anything except my missing brother—not until I see him all in one piece ....

But I also need to make sure I still have a boyfriend. That's the only way I'll survive the next nineteen million, four hundred forty thousand, one hundred seconds of school.

Trust me.

This time, Jared disagrees. "I'm not sure we need to split up." He shoots an angry look at Billy and then looks back at me. "Kelly ..."

I'm not sure I feel better about my nemesis using my correct name for once. He has no right, in fact, to call me anything.

"Let's trust your brother and Casey to figure this out. Let's stay here, all of us, together." Clearly, Jared doesn't have a little brother.

Sarah nods. "Best plan so far."

I can't help myself, my mouth hangs open in astonishment. She *does* have a little brother. He might be a not-so-rabid wolf, but she knows the trouble he and my brother can get into.

She turns to me. "The boys will be fine on their own. This is a big room—it'll take all of us spreading out to notice if one of the machines turns on by whatever the boys do in the control room."

I shut my mouth.

The betrayal is real.

Maybe I'm in the riddle about the farmer who has a chicken, a fox, and a bag of feed on one side of the river, and she has to get everything across to the other side by using a very small boat. She can't take everything in one trip and she can't leave certain things together or they'll eat each other.

Sarah doesn't want the big-rabid wolves left alone together, and Jared, for some stupid secret reason that the wolves haven't revealed, won't let me be alone with the very kissable Billy Fowler.

And everyone seems to trust our little brothers to get themselves back to us without dropping through this evaporating spaceship into endless, airless space.

Is everyone crazy and clueless except me?

CHAPTER 25

HEADING FOR A BREAKDOWN

You probably think that I'm the clueless girl who thinks having a boyfriend will solve all her problems.

I don't.

I've been stronger than I ever thought I could be—just showing my face at school for the past for the past nineteen million, four hundred forty thousand nine hundred seconds.

And I don't want to have to be that strong for even one more second—I'm tired. You'd be tired too.

Tired of the whispers.

Tired of not being able to eat at lunch because your stomach's tied in knots.

Tired of keeping your head down and ignoring everyone around you.

Tired of trying to come across like nothing gets to you.

And failing.

And I've failed at keeping my brother with me and safe on this space ship.

I'm almost in tears. I'm barely holding them in.

It is taking me every ounce of strength to not run up that ladder after my brother.

I should do it. I should leave and I should find my brother.

Or I should just let the tears come.

At least I would feel some relief.

But if Billy is still deciding about whether to date me, I can't cry in front of him because that would make me seem weak.

Or worse, if I do what I want to do and run after my brother, maybe he'd think that I'm super over-protective and that I'll be all clingy in a relationship and why would he want that kind of girlfriend?

Or that I need to be in control all the time and I'd be a controlling kind of girlfriend.

I know that gravy boat looks like it's already sailed, but I need Billy to be my boyfriend.

So that I don't have to be so very strong all the time, and so I can find a tiny pocket of social okay-ness until the limerick is forgotten.

And I also can't go after my brother because my nemesis, Jared Soggy Breadsticks Bilkens challenged me.

Don't I trust my brother?

I can't admit that I really don't.

That he's an-almost-rabid-wolf who needs my protection. Because to the outside world, he's too old to be watched over all the time by a big sis.

Even though he totally needs me to watch over him.

Even though I'm the thing that keeps him safe all the time.

We are on a spaceship, for burned-toast sake.

So I'm rapid-fire blinking to keep in my tears. I mean, I could go and cry in a corner somewhere, but then afterward my eyes would be all red and my face would be all blotchy. The only thing I can do is not start to cry in the first place.

And Jared Bilkens already made me cry enough this year. No more tears. But I'm not really sure I have that kind of control right now.

I no longer care about whatever stupid reason Billy is fighting with Jared.

I don't care about anything at all except seeing my brother again in one piece and getting him off this stupid Easter egg spaceship.

I know that's a lot of stupids all in a row, but that's just where I am.

Sarah bounces up to me, but I shake my head.

She's about to put her arm around me, and I know that if she does, then I will lose my hold on dry eyes.

She understands.

Well, sort of.

She understands because she's my best friend, so she knows what I'm thinking. But I know that she trusts her brother Casey in a way that I can't trust Tim. But also that she thinks that I should trust Tim like that. Not that she really ever criticizes me for it.

You know, best friends don't.

But I can see it in her eyes.

And right now she can see, in my eyes, how close to the edge I am.

I need to stop thinking.

I go through it in my mind one more time.

I can either look like a wussy-over-bearing sister and lose all my credibility with my New Guy or stay and be tortured by the idea of Tim falling out of a hole-y spaceship into space.

I don't even know if staying will help me keep my New Boyfriend.

Billy Hot Cross Buns Fowler answers that for me.

He plants a quick kiss on my cheek and tells me to follow him.

Thank goodness, the gravy boat is still here.

I put my hands up to my face and press it hard to smooth it out. I'm not ignoring that I just kind-of got a kiss from my new boyfriend. I'm just dealing with a lot and it didn't feel the way I thought it would. Maybe if my brother wasn't missing, it would have felt … better.

I look back up the ladder.

Sarah gives my shoulder a shake. An its-going-to-be-okay shoulder shake.

"Okay. Let's look around here and let the boys go back to the command center on their own." Even as I'm saying the words, I can't believe it.

I'm not going with what everyone is saying is the thing to do because of something stupid like peer-pressure. I'm just so tired and so close to a breakdown. It's easier to give in than to be strong right now.

But still.

I feel sick to my stomach.

How did making the wrong choice become the right thing to do?

But once I decide something, I go with it.

So I start to walk around the room and continue to plug things in. It's crazy to think that these machines would ever actually work again.

They crashed down from the room above, are all leaning at weird angles, and I don't even know if I'm plugging things in to the right places.

I'm literally just sticking wires into marshmallow walls.

We're never getting off this stupid Easter egg spaceship.

Sarah works beside me, plugging things in, occasionally looking tenderly at me and giving me worried smiles.

Like she's been waiting for me to break down all year, and now she thinks it's here.

Hell in a bread-basket, *I* think it's here.

She nods and looks over my shoulder, which is my only warning that Billy is there before he wraps his arms protectively around me.

Awesome boyfriend behavior.

I could sink into his embrace and forget all about what's happening—just for a moment.

But I don't have a moment.

The boys have made it to the control room, and we know this because the TV monitor sparks to life once again. This time with sound.

I almost cry in relief. Tim is alive! For the moment.

Billy's arms lock around me as if he's surprised about something. They tighten and press down on me.

"Too tight! That hurts. Let go!" I swivel out of his arms and look at his face.

His mouth is pinched like he's super angry about something.

And I start to process the words coming out of his mouth—not the Billy standing before me in the room, but the Billy trapped in the TV set and yelling from before.

Tim and Casey somehow found the recording of the boys trapped in the marshmallow cell and are playing it back on the TV screen, this time with sound.

Nine-hundred-second-ago Billy is yelling.

Yelling words that I wish I'm not hearing.

CHAPTER 26

ON SUCH A TIMELESS FLIGHT

I've already told you that one of my rules is that it is better to know something than to not know something. Better to look at whatever it is—a grade, a test, a note from the teacher about how I can improve—even if I don't want to look.

Because even though it feels bad in the moment, it doesn't feel as bad as wondering what the grade or test or note really says.

It's better to know.

Except that maybe there are certain people, certain situations that it just makes me feel bad to know about. Maybe some people are specifically toxic to certain others.

Like Jared rock-hard-pancake Bilkins.

Like his limerick.

But, you know.

Train wreck.

I stare at Billy's face and then grab Sarah's hand and station myself directly in front of the TV set.

I hunker down to watch.

In-the-TV Billy turns to look at on-screen Jared. "Somehow, this is your fault!" Completely out of control and yelling. Spitting.

Jared looks puzzled, inspecting his surroundings.

"Where are we?" he asks.

Billy doesn't answer. He scowls.

TV Jared walks his hands over the soft insides. "Walls like an insane asylum. Do you know how you got here? I don't."

"I know *I'm* not crazy." Billy spins around on the spot. "How do you know these walls are like ones in an insane asylum?"

Jared ignores him. "What were you doing before you got here?" Jared now kneels down and inspects the floor, with his eyes and hands.

"Why does it matter what I was doing before I got here?" Billy pushes Jared over.

"Hey, are you four-years-old? Be cool." Jared stands up, and now he glares at Billy. "I just thought that maybe whatever we were doing before we landed here would give us clues as to where we were and how we got here."

"I was riding past Kelly's house on my bike."

"Why were you riding past Katie's house? Can't you leave her alone?"

"You're stupid."

"Luckily I don't care what you think." Jared runs his hands over the walls. He can reach both opposite sides at the same time.

"You know her name's not actually Katie, right? It's a a stupid nickname—everyone thinks so. Everyone thinks you're stupid—do you care about that?" Billy makes fists with his hands.

Jared shrugs.

Even though I hate Jared, (hate is an understatement) I

cringe at the words coming out of my New Boyfriend's TV mouth.

I don't understand why he's acting so terrible. I've never seen him be anything except kind. But to be honest, I've never seen him and Jared together before ever. Maybe they are nemeses.

I turn to watch the real life Jared behind me.

He shrugs, mirroring his shrug on the screen. Then he shakes his head. "Maybe you shouldn't watch anymore," he says to me. He clearly doesn't want to see himself be made fun of from the outside.

But a part of me feels like Jared has it coming.

After what he wrote.

On that blue tile wall.

But does he have to relive whatever humiliation Billy dishes out on this video? I don't think that I could relive the bathroom thing. A picture was bad enough. A video of it would probably destroy me.

And I was pretty destroyed just by that picture.

Which was all Jared's doing.

Come to think of it, he totally deserves anything he gets from my New Boyfriend.

I want to put my hands on my hips and tell him that. Finally stand up for myself.

But my thoughts are interrupted by the recording, and I don't turn it off (I wouldn't know how, honestly) and don't put my hands on my hips. Or stand up for myself.

I'm not sure I'm put-my-hands-on-my-hips girl.

"All you were doing was riding past Katie's house? Just riding past?"

"What were *you* doing before you got here? Giving someone else the all-high-and-mighty third degree?" Billy punches Jared in the stomach.

Hard.

"Stop it," I say, even though this is a recording. And even though it's Jared.

Nobody deserves to be hurt.

On-screen-Jared turns away from the camera.

I turn to my right and stare at Billy. "You punched him."

"It's okay." Jared is so close behind me that I can feel his whisper on my neck.

I shiver.

Tim tells me things are okay all the time, too.

He doesn't mean it either.

He means that I can't change whatever it is that's wrong, and that is the thing that is okay.

Even when it's not.

I can't see Jared's expression on the screen, but I can hear his answer, after he catches his breath. "I was playing solitaire."

"Of course, you were!" TV Billy runs his fingers through his hair, but this time I don't find it all that endearing.

Real-time Jared strides out from behind me. He plants himself right in front of me and waves his hands up and down like he's trying to block me from scoring in a sport played with a ball.

I want to tell him that doesn't work in swimming, which is the only sport I do.

"Let's not watch. Let's go find your brothers in the control room." He waves his hands some more. He must really be embarrassed by what happens next.

I should turn around and walk away, but I can't look away. I want to know what happens.

And, anyway, I can still see the TV set behind him.

I reach out and grab Billy's hand. Mostly so I can pinch him if he's mean again, so he knows I don't like it.

He pulls me closer to him. "We should go. If you want to know what happens on the video, I can just tell you." He flashes a dirty look at Jared.

I can't tell if it's aimed at Real Jared or TV Jared.

Jared's quiet voice on the recording interrupts us. "If I ever find you climbing her tree again, you'll have to answer to me."

Climbing whose tree? Climbing my tree?

What does that even mean?

The tree outside my window?

The tree the spaceship practically landed on?

Oh.

"You climb the tree in my backyard?" I face Billy.

He holds my hand tight.

"Why do you do that?" But I already know, and my face turns beyond red into purple.

The tree outside my bedroom window. Do I close the blinds every time I got into my PJs? No, I don't.

I try to pull my hand out of his hand.

Billy shakes his head. "No, that one time, I was trying to throw rocks at your window to get you to talk to me, when Jared showed up." He holds my one hand in his two.

I stop pulling. Maybe he's telling me the truth. How would Jared know? Clearly Jared doesn't like him.

The smallest voice inside my head says, 'for good reason.'

I ignore it.

Annoying Niggling voice.

Jared's the bad guy here. He's the one who wrote that stuff about me on the bathroom wall.

But Billy's not winning any awards for best grilled-cheese maker right now.

Jared rolls his eyes and moves to the side of the TV

screen. Billy smiles at me and squeezes my hand. But I'm not feeling any electricity anymore.

TV Billy isn't smiling. He's yelling now. "Do you think I even care if you catch me? You and what army are going to make me do anything? We're trapped in this tiny room, and you're trying to teach me manners?"

Real Billy repeats. "I climbed up to throw rocks. It was days ago." He pulls me toward him and away from the TV.

Jared's calm TV voice pulls my attention back. "It might be impossible to teach you manners. But I'll let her know."

TV Billy's face is red and huffing. "I don't even care. She might be cute, but she probably isn't even worth the bother. I'm just getting close to her to make sure she never finds out it was me who wrote that stuff about her on the bathroom wall. You have to admit, it was pretty funny stuff! And if I date her, then I'll have evidence. Proof that the limerick is true. You know: There once was a fish-girl called Kelly …"

That's when Sarah starts talking to me. Just talking.

As if she's been holding words in for as long as I've been pushing the limerick's words off.

Things that don't even make sense. "Looking forward to another grilled cheese when we get home—maybe with bacon? Are you getting enough pool time now that swim is over for the season? What did you choose as a topic for the English assignment? Did you hear that Sally is dating Jack? Well, I don't know if they are official, but they kissed at the baseball game last week. We're supposed to bring drinks to Mike's on Friday, do you think all Coke is okay?"

I can only hear Sarah—I can't hear the rest of the limerick spewed out in the voice of the boy who really wrote it.

It doesn't matter—I know the words by heart.

But I almost can't hear Sarah either—her words sound like they are from some distant planet.

I hear a cat's meow, again from a distant planet, and I'm in a fog and everything is moving in slow motion.

I try to pull my hand out of Billy's grasp, but he won't let go. And then his face looms in front of mine and I get confused and instead see his ranting TV face coming at me. He's leaning in for a kiss, and I can't get away.

I wrench my hand out by twisting hard. "Turn it off, turn it off."

Jared tugs on the cord, trying to turn it off.

Tears roll down my face, and I don't even care. "Turn it off!"

Billy is still advancing on me, I see his mouth moving, but I can't hear the sounds above his other voice ranting about seeing me through my bedroom window and about the stuff he wrote about me on the bathroom wall.

He wrote it.

Not Jared.

My New Boyfriend.

I feel like I'm in a tunnel. I'm hearing things like they're far away and my vision is all fuzzy.

I sit down hard on the floor, just to feel something solid beneath me.

When I do, I remember that the floor isn't actually all that solid.

I can't block my eyes and ears all at the same time so I hold my hands to my ears until real-life Billy's face looms too close in front of me again. Then I block him with my hands.

Someone gently pulls my hands away from my face and Sarah sits down, nose to nose with me. Staring intently in my eyes.

Telling me it's okay.

Out of the corner of my eye, I see that Jared has stopped trying to pull the plug on the TV and has fled the room.

Billy's standing off to the side now, and even though he's pretty calm, all I can see is his TV-ranting face and all I feel is the millions of seconds that I thought he didn't write that awful poem.

I close my eyes to center myself.

It's okay.

But it totally isn't.

Billy's a jerk. His niceness is all fake. The TV is still spewing ugliness.

I stand and push him farther away and put my hands over my ears again, and now I am the four-year-old.

Tears streaming down my cheeks.

My eyes squeeze shut.

Like I'm throwing a tantrum.

But I'm not.

It's the opposite of a tantrum.

I'm seeing—hearing—the truth, about who Billy is.

Someone tugs at my hands. I squeeze my eyes even more shut, if that is possible. "Go away, Billy. Go far away."

I wonder if my tears falling onto the floor are creating enough water to make Billy fall into space.

Deep space wouldn't be far enough away from me.

CHAPTER 27

SYRUP-Y VOMIT SCRAPPLE IN SPACE

I've never heard a voice outside the one in my head recite that poem. And boy, do I hear that poem a lot inside my head. I try not to recite it to myself, of course. But there you go.

Now I only hear those rhyming words in Billy's voice.

He wrote it.

Not Jared.

"Kelly. Are you okay?" Sarah pries my hands off my ears far enough so I can hear her.

I open my eyes. Sarah stands between me and the yelling TV-Billy.

She looks super pissed off. Her eyes are all narrow, and her lips are pressed into a thin line.

Real Billy stands behind us, facing the door, with his hands in his pockets.

Sarah rubs my wet cheeks with her sleeve. "Jared's out there, distracting your brother so he and Casey don't come in here. What the hell is that?" She shakes her head at TV-Jerk Billy. Then at the Jerk Billy in the room.

I shrug.

I know, totally generic.

But words fail me right now.

Jared is keeping my brother from hearing this trash?

It's going to take me a while to start thinking nice things about Jared, but that was a nice thing to do.

I wipe my cheeks with my hand, to get the last little bit of water off.

TV Billy winds down. TV Crumbles winds up.

I take a deep, shaky breath.

The TV screen switches over to fuzz.

Jared pops his head into the door on the same level as us—not the one two stories above. Somehow he's found a new way back to the central room we're in.

He looks everywhere except my face. "Hey gang. Tim, Casey, and I were talking and we had an idea about how to get home, now that um … the machines … are working in here. Well, it's really Tim and Casey's idea, and it's a good one. But we also heard some clanking down the hallway. I'm feeling like we should probably move along."

Home. My face burns when I think about my home with the tree behind it. But then I wonder why *my* face is burning.

Shouldn't Billy be the embarrassed one? He's the one who broke my privacy and invented a nasty rumor about me. A nasty rhyming rumor. One that people couldn't get out of their heads.

I didn't do anything wrong.

"I didn't do anything wrong." I point my finger at shark-bait-chum Billy. "You did."

Okay, I admit, I could probably be more eloquent, but the words still feel really great coming out of my mouth.

Just let that clanking thing come for us, I am angry enough to face anything and tear it apart.

Climbing the tree in my back yard. Writing a slimy limerick. Who does he think he is?

He thinks he's allowed to talk to me, evidently. Because here he is, right in my face again.

"It was only a stupid joke, can't you take a joke?" he asks.

And that's when I boil over. Because the thing that I hate the most, the very most, is when people do something horrible and then pretend that there is something wrong with you because you actually think it's horrible.

"It wasn't a joke. It was mean. It was beyond mean. It was inexcusable. And immature and petty, but most of all unkind. And you are nothing better than vomited scrapple."

Although, I have to admit, I really like scrapple—doused in pancake syrup, that is. But nobody else likes scrapple, and it's kind-of gross, if you think of what it's made of.

Just like Billy. Douse him in the right amount of fake sweetness, and you can mistake what he's made out of.

And right now, you're probably yelling at me a little bit yourself. I'm sure you saw it all along—Jared's done nothing but be kind this whole time, and Billy's been a schmuck.

But you didn't live through the cheese-melting embarrassment and then have the captain of the (JV) basketball team suddenly want to date you.

And you didn't see Jared standing over that limerick, that dirty, disgusting limerick, being egged on by his guy friends.

Standing over that thing with a sharpie.

"Wait." I turn to Jared. "If Billy wrote the … thing … on the bathroom wall, not you, then what were you doing to it?"

I guess I am put-my-hands-on-my-hips girl.

"You thought I wrote it? That explains a bit." Jared smiles shyly at me. "I took the sharpie and blacked the limerick out. But not before someone took a picture of it and shared it." He nods in the direction of Vomit Scrapple.

Oh, of course.

Billy wrote it, photographed it, and shared it with the whole school?

And climbed up the tree outside my bedroom window to further strip me of my privacy?

For a moment I wish that the white pillowy floor would open up and swallow me. Whole. But only for a moment.

For all the moments after that, I wish that the floor would suck down Billy Fowlers.

Again, I wonder, why should *I* feel so embarrassed?

Now I have a nemesis—a real nemesis. "You sit down and don't talk to anyone, until we tell you that you can. I'm just mad enough to melt the ground beneath your feet." I point to an overturned couch, and Billy can tell I mean what I say because without a word he walks over and slumps down.

I glance at the now silent TV set to make sure it doesn't want to reveal anyone else's secrets to me.

A clanking coming from the corridor on our level finally directs my attention to the big picture once again.

We are on a spaceship, with a Clanker coming after us and no way home—yet. "Don't just stand there, shut the door!" I gesture to the less-than-rabid wolves standing just inside the room gaping at me.

They push the door shut.

"So what is this plan you guys came up with?"

Things are starting to make sense again.

Except for one thing.

I don't wait for the boys to answer my question before I turn to Jared Bilkens and ask, "Why, for the love of chicken tenders, do you always call me Katie?"

CHAPTER 28

RAW AND FLATTENED LINGUINI

I know, I know. We're in a melting space ship, my cat is lost, there's a Clanker advancing in the hallway, and I still don't know how I'm going to get everyone home.

Plus, the guy who wrote a raunchy and life-ruining limerick is sitting right over there.

And I'm asking some other guy why he calls me by the wrong name?

I must be clueless.

But I'm not. I just think I might have the wrong feelings.

Has that ever happened to you? There's a misunderstanding, it gets cleared up, but the feelings are left over. The bad feelings. The wrong feelings.

I'd like to clear those up, right now.

My wrong feelings about Jared Bilkens.

I guess it's natural after months of me thinking that he humiliated me so much that I could barely show my face at school, it would take a few moments to de-program my brain.

I'm trying to help it along, by clearing the air.

I'm also wondering how every time I saw Jared, I

thought he was looking at me in a way that matched the terrible bullying.

That he was mocking me, or hating me. Or something.

And he wasn't. He was just looking at me. How wrong I was about how he treated me.

Crusty-moldy-week-old-over-processed-bread Billy Fowler let me think it was someone else this whole time. Then he tried to woo me to keep me from finding out that he did it.

Is 'woo' something people say? My parents say it, but they're rarely a good barometer.

I glare behind me at the couch. Billy sits there twiddling his thumbs and doing nothing at all to help us.

I'm pretty sure that I told him to do nothing, but I can still be mad about it.

My brother doesn't let Jared answer my question, but pulls him (literally, of course) into a conversation at the big white droopy cell.

"Hey." I cross the room and tug on Jared's sleeve.

I feel like dough that has gone through one of those linguini-making presses.

Raw and flattened.

Casey fiddles around with the end of the wires that connect to the big white marshmallow cell, while Tim and Jared discuss, well, me, it seems.

"So, when your sister sat at the control panel, she mumbled my name and you saw my face on a TV screen?" Jared leans against the marshmallow cell and watches Tim squirming around inside it.

Well, Jared watches his lower half, anyway. Tim is lying with his upper half all the way inside the cell.

Tim's muffled voice floats out. "Not just your name and your image. Billy's ...."

But Jared cuts him off with a panicked glance toward me. "Yup, let's not worry about that part of it yet." He looks at my hand tugging his sleeve as if he fears it.

And for some reason, the most important thing right now is to find out why Jared has called me by the wrong name for as long as I can remember.

"Hey," I repeat. I'm trying to get over my hatred of him. It's super weird to try to see him as a good guy.

"Hey," he answers back.

"Hay is for horses and sometimes cows ...."

A swift kick to Tim's feet stop him from finishing his rhyme. Nobody in their right mind should ever repeat any rhymes in front of me ever again.

I'm hoping I can change how I feel about Jared.

I doubt I'll ever feel good about rhyming words in my lifetime.

"You really didn't write that ... thing?" I drop my hand from the tugging, which I'll admit, was probably getting weird. But I need something to anchor me. Otherwise, I'll simply float off into space ....

"I didn't write that thing. Tim, what happened next? After you saw us—me—on the screen?" Jared asks.

Tim shimmies out of the drooping marshmallow. "I don't know. What happened, K?"

I know full well that these guys are trying to get us home, and that somehow they have some awesome idea, and that maybe I should let them take the lead.

Maybe I should let them drive.

But first, "Why do you call me Katie?" I need to know.

"I don't call you Kay-dee." Jared sighs a sigh that let's me know he things I'm a tad crazy for interrupting their get-us-home-now-before-the-Clanker-comes-or-the-spaceship-melts-to-goo discussion.

Which I guess is what it sounds like when I say the name Katie. But still, kind-of rude to correct someone.

Although it is slightly reassuring that Jared is still opposite-guy. At least I haven't been wrong about EVERYTHING regarding him.

"I call you K." He pauses. "T. You know, your initials, as a nickname?"

Ahhh. That makes some sense. Weird, that I didn't ever consider that.

I am nickname-girl after all.

Tim is tapping on Jared's shoulder to tell him something. Something super important, I'm sure. I don't relish the bruise he's probably getting. As you know, I have a matching one on my arm.

"Wait a minute, bud," Jared says, "Let me talk with your sister about something. We'll figure this out in a moment."

Drip-drips ping across the room, and I wonder how many seconds we actually have left to talk.

We should be feverishly finding a way home.

But I'm still in a truth daze.

And I almost got a boyfriend this afternoon—I did for a moment, in fact—but my feelings toward that guy had been so wrong and so misplaced.

And I understand that the plan of get-a-boyfriend-so-everyone-would-know-the-limerick-was-wrong was a good one, and for a split second I wonder if I could transfer that life raft to Jared.

Maybe Jared could ask me out and save me from the social outcasting.

If I could change how I feel about Jared, and quickly, then, honestly, the simplest remedy for social piranhas is to hide behind being a couple. Because his friends would no longer be able to make fun of me—guy code and all—and then those people's friends and so on and so forth, until the entire school just gives up on the bullying, finally.

That's been my plan for a while, but with Billy as the boyfriend shield. Could I switch gears this quickly to Jared?

Jared looks directly into my eyes, and I smile warmly at him, trying to still get over the way I've looked (or avoided) looking at him all year.

"KT?"

"Yes?" Here it comes. The big question. For the second time today—not that the first one counted.

I shove Tim's hand away from Jared's shoulder so Jared won't get off track.

Tim starts tapping me instead.

Ouch.

"I think we could come up with a plan to counteract some of that stupid gossip online, if we really tried hard."

"You do?" What?!

This is not going as I thought it would.

Where's the asking out?

Where's the kiss?

"I do. I can help. Since we're friends now. I didn't know why we weren't friends before. Everything's starting to make sense today." He grins at me and turns to my brother and they start feverishly talking about getting home.

I deflate a little and sag against the marshmallow cell wall.

It's too much to think having a boyfriend would really flip a switch and solve everything. That it would make the whole school forget about the rhyme.

But that's what I desperately need.

The pain to stop.

The memory to just leave the collective consciousness.

Or a time machine to make it so the limerick never appeared on the bathroom wall.

But there's no easy way out.

I finally see that.

Nothing I do can change what people think.

I'm tired. So tired of feeling less than.

Suddenly all I want is to sink through the floor and just keep sinking. Down and down and down.

I want to not be in charge anymore. I want not to have to solve everything.

I'm tired of pretending to be okay with the whole school making fun of me.

Of being okay with hiding at home, watching movies with my little brother.

I'm tired.

I just want to forget it all.

And here I am, on this stupid spaceship. Responsible for my brother. Having (somehow!) teleported others here.

Responsible for getting everyone home.

Dejected, I shrug. "Tim, you think you know how to work this in reverse?"

I'm out of solutions.

Maybe I should let him drive.

CHAPTER 29

TRUTH TRUTH TRUTH

Blah, blah, blah, roses, roses, roses. I know what you're thinking, that suddenly, I could trust my brother and everything is perfect.

I don't know what planet you're on.

Well, actually, I do—the same planet I'm trying to get back to. Earth.

But, everything's not perfect.

My brother is still super annoying.

He's tapping on my shoulder again, so you can take that as case in point.

And there's water streaming down the opposite wall, turning things blue.

Machines are starting to fall down from this level too, and I don't want to go check to see what they are falling into.

Even though we can't hear the Clanker, we know it's out there, and it could find the door any time now.

Maybe the worst thing (well, not to you, but certainly to me) is that I am starving right now.

I get pretty irritated when I am starving. I'm not a

candidate for Survivor, let's put it that way. I turn into a rabid wolf without regular meals and snacks.

"So, if we get this cell working, and we all think hard about going back to Earth, we can use the teleporter in the control room to telepathically send us there."

I know my brother's plan would sound perfectly doable while standing inside the TARDIS, but you know, we're not.

We're standing inside a marshmallow Easter egg spaceship.

"But we're not in the control room, we're here. And I don't think we can get there—with the ship's affinity for melting around us. I don't think we should chance it. We barely got back here." Jared shakes his head.

Like he's found THE ONLY flaw in the plan.

"Didn't you say your sister was sitting at the control panel when the ... teleportation ... happened? And didn't you say it looked like she was stuck to the control panel at the time?"

Rehashing what already happened. Not sure that is going to help us. Ugh. I shake off the impulse to contradict Jared.

Tim shakes his head yes and no at the same time.

Didn't think that was possible?

Meet my little brother, Tim.

And I'm actually impressed that Tim noticed all that was happening to me at that control panel—I hadn't even realized that I spoke any words, but Tim heard me mention people's names.

I rub my stomach to get it to stop rumbling and put my hand onto the soft goo of the cell wall.

"I don't think that we need to be in the control room at all—there are identical controls inside the white cell, here."

Casey shoves his body into the cell and Tim dives in to follow him.

"I'm not sure that's true—I was in that cell for longer than I wanted to be, and I didn't find any controls whatsoever." Jared shouts a little so the boys can hear him.

Tim's head pops back out the mushy melted door. "Oh, we found them, alright. You just didn't look hard enough."

I can't keep myself from muttering low, "He means you didn't touch every inch of everything."

"Yes, that's what I mean!" Tim says brightly from within. It's hard to mock someone who is impervious to mocking.

Sarah smiles at me and puts her arm around my waist. "You okay?"

"I'm okay."

She looks like she doesn't quite believe me.

"Let's get home," I say. If I am going to be not-okay anywhere, I prefer to be not-okay in front of a big, melty, grilled cheese sandwich and a cold can of coke.

My stomach grumbles angrily.

"Come inside, guys!"

Tim's enthusiasm is not catching, but I give him a half smile, anyway.

"No. There isn't room for everyone—I should know, I was in that thing before, and don't want to go back, if that's okay." Jared shakes his head to emphasize his words.

See, Jared really does do the opposite of what everyone asks him to do.

As if to show him how infuriatingly oppositional he is, I scrunch down and push myself through the door, trying to get my completely-normal sized butt in as quickly as possible.

It's a tight fit. My nose is on Tim's sneaker before my

toes are all the way in. And I don't know whether you've had any experience with wolf feet, but pee-yew.

I jump up before I need to inhale.

It's a little like being inside a cloud—or you know, what I thought it would be like inside a cloud the first time I flew in a plane.

What a disappointment clouds are in real life.

But the spaceship cell is soft and warm and fluffy and white.

If really small.

Sarah slides gracefully in, and I help her to her feet (as if she needs the help).

With four of us here, it's really tight.

Like beyond what I think those tiny Chef Boyardee ravi-olis must feel like inside their can.

Sarah takes a deep breath and then sticks her face out the little door hole.

She's not a fan of small spaces, so I hope we don't have to be in here long.

Hopefully a quick demonstration, and then we can head back out into the machine graveyard to let her breathe.

"Casey, how do you know that this is going to work—that it wasn't damaged in the fall?" I ask.

"Hmm. Well, I don't, really. But before, there were only small white lights up there," he points over our heads, "but now there's some yellow ones too. Hopefully that means that there is power to this portal."

"This what?" Jared sticks his head and shoulders into the hole and we all back away to give him room to come in.

We smush into the wall and Tim and Casey push into us.

Sarah automatically puts her arms around Casey and he lets her snuggle him.

I think about doing that with Tim, but he just might karate chop me in response.

I just never know.

Jared stands up and Sarah presses her eyes closed—now there's really no room in here.

"It's a portal. We're calling it a portal. We think that my sister teleported you here because she was thinking about you and ... him. While she was touching the controls. We're going to try to do it again—and teleport all of us home." Tim sounds so adult-like, maybe SS is right that I should give him the benefit of the doubt.

I only turn a little red from his words about who I was thinking about.

But, it's true. While sitting at the control panel, I thought of Billy and Jared.

Vividly.

And then I felt those warm electric fuzzies up my arms. And thought I was being electrocuted.

"Not that I want to stay here for a second more than I need to, but there's something I want to say before we do what we need to do to get home. Something I want to leave up here in space." Sarah squeezes her eyes shut even tighter, but finds my hand and squeezes that too. "Kelly, I've let you wallow all year."

She opens her eyes and sees me getting ready to rebuke her statement. "No, I don't want you to tell me how you haven't been wallowing, how you have been surviving. I know you have. I see you."

She shuts her eyes again and you could hear a pin drop (well, not a pin, since the ground is soft—and getting softer). "You've been counting the seconds since those words were written on the bathroom wall, you've been counting the seconds until middle school is over. It's not about those seconds, though. It's not about time. It's about what you put into that time. The heartbeats, not the seconds. You are walking through time, not putting yourself into it. Not putting your heart in." She takes a shallow, shaky breath, and I marvel at how loud her voice is, not in volume, but in meaning.

Her words are hitting me right in the gut.

"I've missed you this year." She shifts and so I shift, so Tim shifts so, well, you get it. "Casey and I, we've been going through something too. Our parents have, well, decided to get a divorce."

I drop her hand and face the soft wall, tapping it like Tim taps my shoulder. Pushing at it as if I could push right through, not sink into the floor, but walk through the wall.

Disappear.

Become invisible.

Sarah is right.

I already did disappear this year. I disappeared on her.

I did live through seconds, not heartbeats.

I didn't even know my best friend was going through such a hard time.

Nineteen million heartbeats had happened without me doing anything other than existing.

Had happened without me trying to do anything or put anything, good or bad into them.

Had happened without me showing up for my friend.

What would the year have felt like if I had counted heartbeats instead?

If I had not been so self absorbed and saw that my friend was hurting?

Counting heartbeats?

Well, that puts everything into perspective.

I turned and tugged Sarah into a hug. "I'm sorry."

I want to say so much more, but I know that Sarah understands the full extent of my sorry. That I wish this stupid spaceship is a time machine, that now that I know I wish I could go back and insert myself into *her* last nineteen million heartbeats.

I accidentally elbow someone—I'm not even sure who.

But they are mature enough not to say anything, and let me and Sarah have our moment.

It didn't escape me that this is the worst possible place for Sarah to stop and give me this truth. That she is somehow beating her own fear of small spaces to share this understanding of me and our friendship and how I've acting all year.

"You're right. I was wishing the seconds away. But you can't wish time away. I was so self-absorbed." My heart stutters in my chest.

I'm not sure I'm strong enough to count my moments by heartbeats, to put myself back into my life, but I owe it to my best friend to try.

Two heartbeats later, Tim reminds us, "Do we want to live on this spaceship? I don't think so. Go ahead, K." He flips open a mushy control panel in the wall of the marshmallow cell. "Think us home."

Putting everything behind me—the limerick, the wishing that time would just skip forward until everyone got tired of bullying me, the boyfriend scheme, I put my hands on the control panel.

No—not putting those things behind me. Not anymore. Holding them in my heart.

So I can stand up for myself.

So I can be present in my life. For my friend. For my brother.

For me.

My hands stick to the control panel.

Stuck. Stuck. Stuck.

One heartbeat. I think of home.

For the first time in a long time, I want to be there.

I want to be in my life.

I want to show up for my friend.

Another heartbeat.

Home.

Warm electricity zips up my arms like a hug.

I think it again—it's that important. I want to be in my life. Back on Earth. With all the problems and the bullying and the Cokes with Sarah. With the craziness of my brother. With Sarah's problems. I want to help her and know what she's going through.

I want the good and the bad. Well, I don't actually want the bad. But I acknowledge that it happens.

A third heartbeat.

I smile at everyone waiting for something to happen.

Tim, Sarah, Casey, Jared, all scrunched into this tiny cell of a room.

Waiting for me to do the thing I need to do.

And, I'm ready to do it.

Before my heart beats one more time, I make a decision.

I will drive us home.

CHAPTER 30

BEST SOLILOQUY EVER

I immediately think of about ten things wrong with this plan, the first of which happens to be ...

"What if instead of bringing us home, I bring home here?"

My heart starts beating erratically and I want to wish us off this ship, but the fuzzies encasing my arms have disintegrated.

I drop my hands to my side.

What now?

Did you think having an internal epiphany would automatically get us home? That suddenly everything would be grilled cheese and Cokes?

You've read too many books. Watched too many movies.

Yeah, I know, me too.

Because I thought that as well, just two heartbeats ago.

Silence echoes in our tiny chamber—I could have heard that pin drop.

I wonder if a pin would puncture the floor? Would the room deflate?

The appearance of a head in the doorway stops my wondering. About the pin, yes, but also about how to get home.

Billy's bulbous watermelon head starts talking, on the offensive right away. Must be a basketball thing. "I know you guys don't want me here, but even more, I would like not to be here."

Before I can protest, words continue to leak from his mouth.

"You brought me here, I don't know how ...." He pulls one of his arms through the hole so that he can gesture rudely to Tim and Casey who look like they want to offer up the answer. "However it happened it was totally your fault. I don't want to be left behind when you guys fly this capsule home."

I awkwardly (it's so crowded it's almost impossible to move in here) turn my head to look at Tim, who is bursting at the seams to correct Billy's incorrect assessment of how we are getting home.

Billy pushes his way into the space, and Sarah's eyes get all big and white.

She mmm's and I can't imagine how claustrophobic she must feel. I scrunch my arm behind Tim, making the soft wall bend so my hand can find hers and grasp it tightly.

But I must have misinterpreted the feeling behind her sounds, because she starts yelling (softly, as only Sarah can) at Billy Week-Old-Sushi Fowler.

"Just because *YOU* would leave US here doesn't mean that we would do the same to you. Even though you made my best friend's year a LIVING HELL and then, as if to add insult to injury, pretended as if you had nothing to do with it, pretended to support her! Nobody here has done anything remotely mean to you in return. Does that tell you anything at all, Billy Fowler?"

Jared nods appreciatively.

"Just because *YOU* would leave *US* stranded on a spaceship, doesn't mean we plan to do that to you. Now sit down and shut up so we can try to get us home." Sarah's lips push into a perfect straight line.

My bottom lip drops open.

Third time today that Sarah's gone into soliloquy mode. She's said more words in the last thousand heartbeats than probably in the past nine million combined.

Go Sarah!

Billy Moldy Bread Fowler pulls his legs in, crawls into a corner, and sits criss-cross-applesauce against the wall. He even turns away from us. I hope we've heard the last of him. I have work to do.

"So, back to my question—when I thought about ... them ... I brought them here. What if when I think about home, I bring the whole house here?"

Now Sarah's intake of breath is definitely out of claustrophobia.

No way could the house fit in this cell with us.

What would happen?

It would probably fall through this soggy spacecraft into the depths of space and pull us with it.

Now that I've covered the worst thing that could happen, it's all I can think about.

But not so my little brother.

"Okay, let's think ...." It doesn't help my worst-thing-that-could-happen-generator that Tim is fiddling with some little controls on that panel folding out from the wall like a laptop. "Instead of thinking about bringing the house to you, think about all of us being inside the house."

Makes sense, except ...

"The first time, I wasn't thinking of bringing Billy and Jared here, though. I was just thinking of them." I inch around the cell so that my back is against the wall and not facing my little brother.

There's barely enough room for all of us to stand shoulder to shoulder, even with Billy Chocolate-Filled-With-Insect-Parts (you know every chocolate bar has some right?) Fowler sitting on the floor.

"Maybe a house is too big to move telepathically, anyway. Did you feel any pain at the time?" Casey weirdly sounds just like my pediatrician.

I think back to that moment when I saw the image of Jared and Billy on the screen in the control room. "I didn't feel any brain pain—if that's a thing—or a headache or anything. In the movies, people always get a bloody nose from overstraining their mental capacity. Nothing like that happened. But I did feel a weird electrical surge through my arms—like my arms were asleep and had pins and needles. And I couldn't move my hands from the control panel— they were stuck. Just for ...."

Water dripping sounds just outside the door makes me forget what I was saying. I duck my head to peek out— water is pooling in the doorway. And the wall around the hole we climbed through is turning blue.

For the love of Saltines-Covered-with-Nutella-and-Cream-Cheese, we don't have any time to talk about this.

Not just Sarah is on the same wavelength as me— everyone (except for Billy Anchovy Fowler) thinks the same thing at the same moment.

"Get over here, K. Put your hands back on the controls and think us back to Earth. Now!" Tim shuffles to one side and pushes on Casey, so we all start moving in a tight circle

(I admit, I 'accidentally' step on Billy Bert's-Every-Flavor-Booger-Flavored-Bean Fowler as I pass), until I am standing at the controls.

I put my hands on them. I don't really think this is going to work. It didn't work one hundred heartbeats ago. But everyone looks at me expectantly.

I hope the Coke gods are listening.

I put my hands on the control and think about home.

Heartbeat after heartbeat.

Desperately.

CHAPTER 31

CLANKER TOAST

Okay, so it's kind-of stupid, that I think that just by touching some buttons and thinking us home for a second time, (in case you forgot that I've already tried this) we will be transported there.

Really stupid.

What's the definition of crazy? Doing the same thing and thinking you'll get a different outcome?

I'm definitely crazy at this moment.

And we are well past grasping at milkshake straws.

I open my eyes to see the blue color creep up the wall.

It's now or never. Everyone is counting on me to save them.

I move my hands over the control panel and shut my eyes again.

I try to feel how things had felt when I first teleported people.

I try to be my brother, ignore the sights and sounds, and just feel, through my fingers, everything about the control panel.

Each time my heart beats, I focus more and more on just feeling.

I move my hands around until the noodle-buttons feel familiar. Then I start thinking. Imagining us home. All of us inside my kitchen (not my kitchen teleported here, please not here!) sitting around the table.

The bright yellow colors of the kitchen wall fill me with a sense of peace—all I've been seeing are pastels and whites and baby-blues since we've been on this ship.

I imagine the way the sun streaks through the window —that will keep the house from coming here, right?

Unless the whole Earth and Sun get transported onto this ship too.

Shut up, worst-case-scenario generator. Shut up, Annoying Niggle.

I take a deep breath and feel Sarah grab my arm, and Tim cover my bruised shoulder with his palm.

Sarah whispers, "You can do this!" into my ear.

And, you know, I'm a pretty dependable person. That's a given. But my confidence has been rocked this year. Not that I think that the limerick is true, or anything—it's not.

But if every room that you walked into for months contained people whispering and pointing, laughing under their breath, or every time you opened an email or went online, you had to prepare for mean and hateful words written about you, you'd lose your sense of who you are too.

All year, I have tried to shove the stuff people say out of my head, but it keeps leaking in.

Until now. There's no room for self-doubt.

I have to transport six people (and a cat! Where is Crumbles?) off this Easter Egg spaceship and back home to Earth.

The water level is rising. I hear nearby machines plummeting through the floor and this portal might be the next to go.

"You can do it," Tim repeats Sarah's whisper to me.

I have to transport us home.

I picture each of us sitting around our breakfast nook. Just sitting. (Well, except Billy Soggy Rice Pudding Fowler, who's never invited into our kitchen.)

I think of the sunlight and the warmth.

Things I haven't felt since we've been on this ship. Hard floors. Hard seats just the right size for human butts.

Laughter.

A sound outside the portal and across the room interrupts my focus.

A deep clanking—clank-clank-clank—moving in our direction.

Whatever it is that has pursued us this whole time on this ship has finally found us. We have nowhere to go.

I try to get back my mental picture of us in my kitchen.

Clank-clank.

Us. In. The. Kitchen.

Clank-clank.

It's no use, I can't focus while that clanking is coming for us. We're sitting ducks in this tiny cell.

Trapped. Trapped. Trapped!

Annoying Niggle is back. 'You failed,' it tells me.

'Everyone is going to die, and it's all your fault,' Worst-case-scenerio generator gets into the game.

And the worst thing is, I know it's right.

We're Clanker toast.

Grilled with butter and grape jelly on top.

CHAPTER 32

ELECTROCUTION ALIEN STYLE

I don't know how you act under pressure, but I pride myself in being cool. You seem like you'd be pretty cool too.

But, you've never been in a wet portal light-years from home, in deep space, trying to transport six people (and a missing cat!) back to earth with intense mental focus while a Clanker comes to eat you.

Cool is not possible in this situation, let me tell you that, right off the bat.

"KT ..." and I totally don't mind Jared using my nickname—he's literally in our circle now. "... it's okay, focus."

But I'm thinking of anything but getting us home.

My brain is misfiring.

Clank-clank.

I think about how I can't call Casey by his initials (CS) because I exhausted all the through-the-wardrobe jokes a long time ago. Plus, don't you think I have enough fantasy in my life through Tim's escapades?

Clank-clank.

I also don't call Tim by his initials—because I'm not

that mean. TT would be a tough one to live down. (If only his middle name started with an N, then it would be the coolest nickname ever, but our parents didn't have that kind of foresight.)

And the whole purpose of calling someone by a nickname is to show you know them, better than anyone, and think they're cool.

Clank-clank.

I think about how, on the Amazing Race (boy have I watched a lot of movies and tv shows during the last nine million heartbeats), it's annoying when other people back-seat drive as someone is doing an individual challenge. But how right now, I'd love for someone to weigh in.

I'd love for this not to be an individual challenge.

Clank-clank.

"What makes home, home?" Sarah's voice is so high that I'm surprised the wolf-boys aren't the only ones who can hear it. But I hear it too. Sun-Young's voice. Because she is the sun to me, and I need to bring her home to our warm kitchen with the sun shining in.

Clank-clank-clank.

Home. Mom and Dad. Tim causing trouble. Our cat. Oh, Crumbles! Crumbles will be lost forever in space. I push the thought away. I can't think of something sad now.

Home. The best part of home. Sun sitting in our kitchen eating grilled cheese, gooey and warm from the griddle. I can smell it.

An electrical charge buzzes in the portal. Grabs my hands and holds them.

"That's it, K!" Sarah's hand presses mine harder onto the panel. I wonder if she can feel the current.

Clank-clank.

Annoying Niggle weighs in. 'What if you transport

everyone except for you and then you get eaten by the Clanker?' Shut up, AN. Shut the blueberry-banana pancake up.

I squeeze my eyes extra tight.

Other hands cover mine and I know without opening my eyes which fingers are Tims, which are Caseys, and which are Jared Red-Bug-Juice Fowler.

I smell grilled cheese frying in our kitchen for me and Sun and Casey and Jared.

Tim will have the macaroni and cheese that steams on the stove.

A just-opened, cold can of Coke fizzes in front of me at the table.

I feel the droplets of spray hit my chin.

Crumbles curls up on my lap, pushing my hand with her head.

Clank-pause-clank.

The thing is right outside our door.

My hands buzz with electricity and become glued to that control panel—maybe this is working!

The portal's floor squish beneath my feet. No time to waste. And suddenly Crumbles is sitting on top of our hands, inside the marshmallow cell.

Her fur tickles my thumbs. My eyes flip open. "Grab her, Tim!"

With a huge meowrooow, Crumbles jumps off our hands and toward the door.

But Tim's lightning fast reflexes have been training for this moment his whole life.

He grabs our cat and folds the bundle of claws and hisses against his chest.

I close my eyes again, feeling awash with satisfied warmth.

For the first time in an extremely long time, I feel like maybe everything will be okay.

My hands are still glued to the control panel. And I press on. Smelling the grilled cheese, feeling the Coke, hearing the voices of my friends and brother in my head.

In between my heartbeats lives the perfect moment, regardless of what is happening at school.

The perfect moment and it makes me so happy.

The floor dips and I can't help but look down, even though I should be keeping my eyes closed.

I'm still thinking and smelling and feeling that moment, but I am also seeing something which is now inside the portal with us.

A little robot-alien with long metal fingers, who has jumped off another metal thing and left it outside the door. Its boxy head considers us all, and a long, pointed finger reaches up, like the metal alien's going to tell us to phone home.

Billy Ant-Eaten-Watermelon-Rind Fowler is the one who screams.

Loudly.

Half my mind is at home in my kitchen, so I'm having trouble understanding what is in front of me, which is probably why I don't react when the alien's finger jabs at me.

That and because my hands are stuck to the control panel.

I don't even need to close my eyes again to see my kitchen in front of me, as a shimmery haze inside this white cell, when the alien's metal finger stabs into my arm.

Warm electrical fuzzies zip from the needle-like puncture up one arm, pausing for a moment at the Tim-bruise on my shoulder, heating it up, then down through my cavernous stomach, through my feet and simultaneously up to the other shoulder and down that arm until I'm one big buzzing bundle of electricity.

In my mind we're all in my kitchen eating gooey goodness.

In my body, I'm burning up like the Clanker's set me on fire.

And then as quickly as the stabbing current came into me, it's gone.

And in reality, real reality, we *are* in my kitchen, standing around my table.

Every single one of us, except for one exception.

I don't see Billy Haggis Fowler anywhere.

I do see a small metal alien in my kitchen, sitting at my breakfast nook.

CHAPTER 33

CATASTROPHIC SOGGINESS

We're home.

Relief doesn't begin to cover it.

The nightmare is over.

Except that it isn't, really.

Because now I'm wondering if I'm the kind of person who would strand a guy on an evaporating spaceship because he ruins (and you know exactly how much he did ruin) my year.

I always thought I was a nice person, but Billy Fruitcake Fowler isn't anywhere to be seen.

You could think five out of six people (plus our cat!) saved would be enough, but you'd be wrong.

I'm also wondering if the Clanker will eat us for lunch.

Although, now, in the bright yellow sunlight of my kitchen, the scary metal Clanker looks a lot like a small friendly robot joining us for lunch.

A big part of me wants to ignore the alien robot and not care about what type of person I am, or who's missing.

That part of me just wants to make a grilled cheese sandwich.

I cross the kitchen and grab a bunch of Cokes out of the fridge as a compromise.

See, nice person.

I throw a Coke to everyone in the room—we've earned it.

Credit.

Tim drops our cat and catches the soda.

Crumbles streaks from the room, looking for the underside of a bed, I bet.

"You did it!" SS is the first to cheerlead my teleportation skills.

Then the metal alien hops down from the breakfast nook bench with a clank.

I shove Tim behind me and back away.

But Tim, ever the alien diplomat, scoots in front of me and raises his hand up in a wave.

"Hello, welcome to our home."

Walking across the kitchen tile floor, the thing clanks just like it did on the spaceship when it was the top half of a double-decker alien.

Clank. Clank. Clank.

It stops a couple feet from us and pushes a button on its front metal panel. "Hello, Earth helpers! Have you seen my mother?"

Without missing a beat, Tim answers the weird metal alien's completely benign question. "No, does she look like you?"

"A slightly larger version of me, yes." The alien holds the button down while he talks to us.

Even though he's metal and his voice sounds like a robot, I can tell that he's sad. His voice has a somber metal twinge to it. "She fell out of our spaceship this morning. Something happened and our spaceship got ... gooey."

Oh, yeah. That was my fault.

I step forward to say so.

Jared puts out his hand (always the disagree-er) and stops me.

Under his breath he says, "First alien on Earth and you want to start the communications by explaining how you wrecked their ship with a hose?"

How on Earth did Jared know about the hose?

My little brother has a big mouth.

What else did he tell him?

Maybe Jared is right, though. But if the robot-alien asks point-blank, I'm going to totally be honest.

I'm a big enough person to fess up to the bad stuff I've done.

I look behind the kitchen bar to see if Billy Burnt Crouton Fowler is there.

He's not.

Neither is a mommy metal alien. No beings behind the bar.

Tim notices me looking and tells our new alien friend, "We're missing someone also. Have you seen a boy the size of him?" He points at Jared.

I think that's being generous to Jared, since the guy we lost is much bigger than him. But I let it go.

I start to sweat. What if I left my nemesis behind? I'm going to have to tell his parents, and it's going to sound unbelievably ridiculous.

He's going to die on that spaceship.

"I can scan for more human life forms." The robot-alien touches another button and scans—us.

The air gets all translucently rainbow ish, just like it did on the ship.

"Nope, no other human forms in this abode."

Drat. I did leave him on the ship.

My mind is going a million miles a minute. I take a step toward the robot-alien.

"Hello, I'm Kelly." I've found it always helps to start by introducing oneself. I think I learned that politeness from my best friend. "I think we left our ..." I can't get the word friend out of my mouth. "... human being on your ship. Can we get him back somehow?"

Lots of lights and buzzers blink rapidly on the alien's front plate. "I'm sorry, due to catastrophic sogginess, my home ship has already fallen apart. Once I find my mom, we'll salvage what we can."

Oh no. Not only did I do exactly what Sarah said I was too nice to do, leave Billy behind, but now he's gone? I can no longer think the word 'dead.'

Catastrophic sogginess. Oh, my charred marshmallows. Well, more like waterlogged marshmallows.

The blood drains from my face.

"My mom will call my dad's ship down to pick us up, but I need to find her—I hope she hasn't left without me!"

He sounds like a very young alien.

I say 'he' because this alien is so clearly a rabid wolf. Getting separated from his mom and following us around a spaceship all day.

"I'm sure she hasn't." Tim walks to the alien and tries to pat him reassuringly on the top of the head.

His hand slaps down, and we hear an echo as if the alien kid is built like a tin can.

Chef Boyardee.

My brain completely shorts out. Not from all the electrocutions I've lived through today, but from the idea that maybe my bully didn't live though this day.

I could have saved him and didn't.

"Moms don't leave Earth without their kids." Jared's voice is completely relaxed like he's not concerned at all, about anything.

Humans shouldn't leave spaceships without their fellow humans.

I guzzle my Coke, so I won't puke.

As I've said before, Coke has magical properties. It doesn't seem to be working right now, however.

Billy deserved a big crash.

But being left for dead in space?

Even Billy didn't deserve that.

CHAPTER 34

I DON'T DESERVE GRILLED CHEESE

I don't know if you've been keeping up with current events, but I just left someone to die in space.

And you know, by now, what my impulse is when I'm feeling sad or ashamed. I like to crawl into bed and be distracted by a good movie.

I mean, I know I've shown you a pretty good side of myself during this day, spouting wisdom like, it's better to look at a problem head-on, etcetera.

But now you know the long and short of it.

Mistakes were made.

Someone wrote terrible things about me and spread it around school. I suspected the wrong person. I decided to date the person who wrote those terrible things. And then I made horrible decisions that cost that person his life, and now all I want to do is go stick my head in the sand.

Or at least into a kinda suspenseful scary space movie, so I can stop feeling what I'm feeling.

What I'm feeling is totally responsible. Yeah, I know 'responsible' isn't really a feeling, but isn't it though?

Only now I think I'd rather watch a chick flick. Seems safer.

But overall, that's the kind of person I am.

I don't blame you if you don't like me—I don't like me all that much right now.

And I don't give my brother enough credit.

Because in this heartbeat, I can see that he knows a bit of what I'm going through. He's watching me carefully, and he and Sarah are blocking my escape route to my bed and TV. Because of course, Sarah knows too.

Casey is busy taking pictures of the alien.

I don't even care. It's not like I'm in charge of protecting human-kind from knowing the truth—that aliens exist.

And who would believe the pictures are real, anyway? The robot-alien looks a little like someone's elaborate science fair project.

Billy is dead. I'm responsible, and nothing else matters.

I toss my empty Coke can in the general vicinity of the recycling bin and walk toward the human fence that is my brother and best friend.

"Let me through."

"No. We need to help our alien friend." Tim gestures behind me. Now the alien pipes up.

"Oh, thank you, kindly!" He clunks across the floor. Are all aliens polite, like Franc and this little guy?

I don't even know what time it is on Earth, so I glance at the microwave. Four thirty.

Mom will be home from work shortly. I can't even think about what she's going to find in the back yard. Lots of damage and wires down. But the microwave still has power, so maybe it's not too bad.

"I'm all helped out." I push my hands between Sarah and Tim and try to pry them apart.

They can't stand in the doorway forever.

"I'll make you a grilled cheese." Sarah smiles.

"I don't want grilled cheese."

Tim gasps at my statement. He's such a happy kid, he can't imagine how sad I can get.

"Yes, you do!" Sarah's voice is falsely cheerful. "I'm not leaving until you have a grilled cheese and until we find our alien friend's mom."

Because those are two equally doable things.

I want to mock her. And she's my best friend.

See, terrible person.

I also note she doesn't say '… and find Billy.' She knows too. He's … gone.

Instead of mocking her, I turn around, slump down into a chair, and put my head onto the table.

"It's all my fault. I killed him." If they won't let me go wallow in the peace and quiet of my own bedroom, then they can just deal with whatever I do next.

Belligerent doesn't look awesome on me, I'm sure.

"It's not your fault—no way." At least Jared is consistent. If I say the sky is blue, he'd probably say it's translucent. And have some stupid scientific fact to back it up.

"Maybe he's not dead. Maybe Franc helped him." Tim is so optimistic.

Franc. What was Franc's deal? He acted all afraid of the clanking alien. Just an alien child looking for help.

Clearly I want to spread the blame around.

"Hey … friend." I don't know how to address an alien, and calling him alien or robot seem kind-of rude. "Do you know Franc? He was on your spaceship. He seemed afraid of you?"

I'm trying not to be interested in anything, but I can't

CHAPTER 35

MISTAKES, MERMAIDS, & MEMES

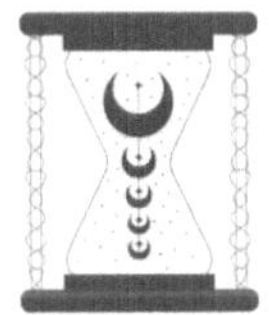

My parents think it's super funny that whenever they offer me the choice to choose my punishment for whatever mistakes I make, I choose something worse than what they would choose for me.

But I know there is no punishment worthy of the damage I've caused today.

The sun's heat hits me hard as I step out the back door, and I notice all the earth things that I missed (but didn't know I missed) on the spaceship.

The sounds of birds calling to one another. The smell of spring. Of warm earth. A train whistle in the distance. A car chugging down the street.

The sun glints off the mother robot-alien so brightly the glare hurts my eyes.

Rabid-wolf robot steps out the door behind me. "Mom!"

The mother turns to look at us and literally shakes the earth with her pounding feet to get to her son. "Belug! You're alright!"

She picks him up and holds him on her shoulder, while beaming at his face the whole time.

"These Earth Friends brought me home." He waves his long thin fingers at us.

"Thank you." She only has eyes for her son.

I wait for Belug to rat me out, but he just cuddles into his mom (as much cuddling as metal on metal can do—if I didn't think it rude I would cover my ears to block out the screeching metal sounds).

In a thunderous voice, Belug's mom yells at our tree. "This does NOT let you off the hook, Earthling!"

I walk to the base of the tree, and who do I see, way up in the top branches, hanging upside-down by his belt, but Billy Still Alive Fowler.

I'm speechless.

Jared is not. "How's the view up there, now, Billy?"

I did not kill my nemesis.

Let me repeat that. I did not kill my nemesis.

I'm not leave-your-nemesis-on-a-melting-spaceship-to-die girl.

I'm the much cooler hang-your-nemesis-in-the-very-tree-he-tried-to-peep-at-you-in-as-payback girl.

My face breaks into a wide grin.

"Can someone get me down?" Billy asks from up in the tree branches.

"NO!" All of us yell.

He can just hang up there and think about how he should treat other people.

I turn to the mother robot-alien. "I'm sorry, I got your spaceship wet today. I was trying to make sure the helicopter didn't start a fire."

"I fell out because my spaceship was wet." She squeezes

the little robot-alien around the waist. "I almost lost this little guy."

Belug shakes his head at his mom. "She brought us back here. She brought *me* back here."

I open my mouth to correct him—after all, I didn't mean to bring him back—at the time, I was afraid of him.

Jared grabs my hand and pulls me back a step. His meaning is clear—don't mess up the first relations with an alien.

So, I don't fess up to that. But I do say, because it's also true, "Belug helped us get back too." I put my hand over my arm, where Belug jabbed me. "He used some kind of electric current to help transport us back."

Credit.

Belug smiles proudly. "I did. I jacked up her electrical circuits to give her the juice to send us wherever she was thinking, which, was back to you." More snuggling.

More ear-bending screeches.

"You didn't know about the wet, dear, I'm sure. And, I guess I've been yelling at that Earthling in vain. I thought he knew where Belug was."

Before any of us can tell her not to, Belug's mom extends her hand all the way up to where Billy Upside-Down-Delivery-Pizza-Stuck-to-the-Top-of-the-Box Fowler hangs. She wrestles him free of the branch and puts him down gently, right-side up.

"You guys are crazy," he yells as he runs out of my back-yard and down the street. He doesn't run all that fast—he's no swimmer.

"It's all really Franc's fault—he knew that he would crash us if he kept popping in and out. But he doesn't like to be alone. He needs to be around beings. He can't help himself." Belug's mom pushes some buttons on her metal chest and then speaks quietly to herself.

We all just stand and watch.

When she finishes, she pats her son on the head mid-snuggle. "I've called your father, and he's coming to pick us up. Maybe your Earth friends should wait inside to avoid another wet issue."

I'm a big fan of people being direct, so I appreciate her words.

Tim bounds up to the robot-aliens. "Bye, Belug! See you soon!"

I'm hoping that we won't see him soon.

The hose is lying against the tree trunk, still pumping water into the grass, so I walk to the spigot and turn the knob until the it stops, not even wanting to think about the amount of water streaming out all day long.

I survey the backyard as we file into the house. It looks smaller than I remember. I guess everything on Earth will seem a little smaller now that I've seen space.

Even the mess in the backyard doesn't seem all that big. There's only one wire down and tons of tree branches lying on the ground. I probably need to call the police about the wire. Maybe I'll let my mom do that when she gets home.

I'm done with being in charge, at least for a little while.

I close the back door behind us.

"Hey, your picture is getting a ton of high-fives online!" Jared offers me Casey's phone, and I take it to inspect a not-too-terrible picture of me with my arm around a robot. It looks like I'm smiling sarcastically, and I have to admit, it's pretty awesome.

As I watch, the image gets a few more high-fives from people I know at school.

It's doesn't erase the whole limerick, but maybe it's a start.

Jared must read my mind (and his telepathy must be immune to his disagreeing-reflex) because he flashes me a grin and says, "It's a start."

Those words mean something to Casey and Tim, who look like they exchange a telepathic thought as well, and dash up the stairs. I can hear them turn the wrong way to go to Tim's room and they slam the door open to my room.

I'm too exhausted to yell at them to respect my privacy.

But they're back before I can crack open another Coke.

Tim carries the toy car with him, and Casey shoves his laptop in front of me. Then he nods to Tim.

"So, in the, uh, the poem ..."

Oh jeez. Of course my little brother saw the limerick. Here I thought I had been protecting him. Clearly I forgot he has the internet, too.

My face flushes. So embarrassing.

Tim swallows, inspects my face, and then continues, "The author mentions the mermaids painted on your bedroom wall."

Yes. My mermaid mural. The mural that Sarah sketched and we both filled in with paint, years ago, when we were into things like that. Sarah trusting me with a paint brush only after she made it a paint-by-number project.

Even though she and I have grown out of mermaids (kind-of, I mean, do you ever really outgrow mermaids? Especially when you're a swimmer?) I couldn't imagine painting it over, because my best friend designed and drew it, and plus, mermaids.

Everything about the limerick was embarrassing—it insinuating that I slept with everyone?

Embarrassing.

It insinuating that I had mermaids on my bedroom walls?

Embarrassing in an entirely different way.

And it's why I feel so caught in it.

Embarrassed about still feeling like a kid. Embarrassed about people thinking I might be not-so-much a kid anymore.

"So, we left devices to record video from inside your room, thinking that the bully was somehow seeing into your window."

This whole time that I have been so self-absorbed, focused on nothing except myself and my own stupid problems, this whole time that Sarah and Casey have been going through their parents splitting up?

This whole time, Sarah has been supporting me. Casey and Tim have been trying to help me. Everyone has been focused on me.

I have been focused on no-one. Except me.

What have I been doing? I've been trying to get someone, anyone, to date me.

As if a stupid, wrong-reason relationship would solve all my problems.

Instead I should have been digging deeper into the authentic relationships I already had.

I put my head down. How awful of me.

"You guys should leave. I've been so focused on myself, I don't deserve you all. I wrongly accused you of bullying me, Jared. I didn't even notice that my best friend was going through some big stuff. I didn't think about how my moping affected my little brother, and you, Casey." I push the Coke away.

I don't even deserve bubbly goodness.

"Well ..." Tim's voice falters.

"Hey, now." Sarah slips into the bench beside me. But she seems at a loss for words too.

"You didn't accuse me—I mean not out loud! Just in your head. And what Sarah told you in the teleport booth? She kept her thing from you because she was trying to protect you. But had she told you about their parents splitting up, what would you have done?" Jared can't not be oppositional.

(Thanks, Franc, for the English lesson.)

But Jared also makes some good points.

I turn to Sarah and give her a big hug. "Let's do something fun," I tell her. "Distract you from the hard stuff."

"Exactly. We're here because you are a good friend. You've been going through something hard. We didn't know how to help you. I still don't." Sarah hugs me. Emphatically.

"Well, that's what we want to show you." Tim nods to Casey.

Casey leans into the booth and clicks play on a video queued up on his laptop.

The video shows Billy, in the tree outside what is clearly my room, mermaids and all, and I have the sinking suspicion an airborne toy helicopter has recorded this view. A helicopter which, I don't know for sure, might be hanging out in space right at this very moment.

In the video, Billy slinks onto the branch closest to my window and holds his phone up at the perfect position to take invasive photos.

I close my eyes. If it hadn't been so long since our grilled-cheese breakfast, I would spew bread and cheese all over this kitchen. My stomach rolls and rolls.

When I can safely open my mouth again, my voice

sounds like it comes from inside a long hollow bucatini noodle. "Why did you want to show me this?"

Tim points his finger and nods again to Casey, who clicks to a second window on his computer.

It's a page full of different moving, as well as static, memes of Billy. Some of the captions are simply, 'Peeping Billy.' Some are worse.

I sit back, away from all the moving Billys in front of me.

"We'll post all these, and he'll get a taste of his own medicine." Tim opens up Blur. Poised to post the memes on the social media platform everyone at Hillside uses.

Suddenly, I know I'm in the driver's seat.

The best driver's seat of all.

Ready to give Billy a taste of his own foul-tasting medicine.

CHAPTER 36

AND FINALLY GRILLED CHEESE

I pinch my eyes shut. I don't know what I want, but I know if we post these memes, the feelings I have will continue. The limerick won't die, it'll keep living on, and my nemesis will experience the same kind of bullying.

I kind-of want Billy to experience it.

But that's the weird thing. Billy has already lived through that kind of bullying.

It's why I thought there was no way he could have written that stupid poem.

A rumor had circulated in sixth grade, which I certainly don't need to repeat, which had earned him the nickname Billy the Bed-Wetter.

"He already has had a taste of his own medicine." I once watched a movie which was pretty good, but also ended with the idea that people sometimes want others to feel the same pain they feel. Hurt people hurt people, a character in the movie had explained.

I scan the faces in front of me. If I could use a shared adjective to describe each of them, the word I would use would be kind.

All three of them, well, four, now that I know that Jared has never hurt me, are more kind than I'll ever be.

And all four of them are poised to do this mean thing. This thing that will make Billy-the-bully feel the pain I've been feeling all year.

Before I fell into the spaceship, before we fell back out again, and before I thought, for a good hundred heartbeats, that I had inadvertently killed my bully, I would totally have pushed publish on those memes.

But now I'm not so sure. I don't know why Billy did it. I'm not sure I believe that people want others to feel as bad as they do, like that movie says, but how many times has Tim passed me food and said, 'this is awful, try it?' So maybe there is something to that idea.

Why-ever he had done it, I don't want to do it, even to him.

But it's more that that. I don't want my kind friends to do something this mean on my account.

"I think I have a better idea." Because while I don't want to ruin his social credit, I do need him to stop climbing the tree behind my window.

Immediately.

Quicker if that's possible.

I press print on one of the static pictures with the words 'Peeping Billy' on it. I run into my mom's office, grab the printout, and stuff it into an envelope, addressing it to Mr. and Mrs. Fowler, and hand it to Jared. "Would you mind sticking this in his mailbox, on your way home?"

"No problem."

And it finally did feel like no problem.

My bully would have to answer to some of his actions, and to grown-ups, no less. If his parents didn't take care of the peeping, then I could slip a picture to the police or tell my parents. But hopefully it wouldn't come to that.

I think of my nemesis high-tailing it out of my yard and smile.

I look at Sarah, really look at her, for the first time in a long time.

She smiles, but the smile doesn't reach her eyes. She's been going through things, and I haven't been there for her.

But that stops in this heartbeat.

Maybe it *is* all about one heartbeat at a time.

I look at Tim, and no longer see all the crazy stuff he's done in his life wrapped up into a walking catastrophe.

He might leap before he looks, but he also laughs with abandon and is the first to see the good in, well, everyone. I have no doubt he has been supporting Casey through Casey's hard times.

I'd be a better friend all around if I took my lead from my little bro.

Maybe I will even take Sarah to Mike's party. And bring a few different kinds of soda, not just Coke. Help Sarah have a fun distraction from what's happening at home.

After all, I had been wrong about Jared. Maybe I had been wrong about other people too. Maybe every time I walked into a class, people hadn't been laughing and talking about me.

And maybe it didn't matter if they did. I mean, you know what I mean.

After all, I know the truth. My friends and family know the truth.

And there are so many real problems in the world, like being stuck on an oozing spaceship somewhere in the galaxy, or having your parents get a divorce; I don't need to hold onto a made-up one.

I listen carefully to my heartbeats. Marking this moment in time.

Going to school will still be hard. There will still be days it feels impossible.

But I can focus on my heartbeats and be grateful for my friendships with the kindest people I know: Sarah, Tim, Casey, and now Jared.

I walk over the to fridge and pull out the cheese and butter.

"Anyone for grilled cheese?"

A NOTE FROM THE AUTHOR ABOUT BULLYING

Bullying is serious.

Anyone who tells you otherwise either hasn't experienced it or isn't being truthful.

Whether it's in rhyme, on the internet, or in person, bullying is awful.

Because everyone is different, and thinks differently, different things help people get through the trauma of bullying.

In this book, the main character, Kelly, tries a bunch of things, including:

- Ignoring it.
- Escaping into fiction—movies, shows, and books.
- Turning to friends for support.
- Helping others with their problems.
- Finding perspective through travel (in space!).
- Understanding that there will come a time when people will forget about the limerick.

We can thank the LGBTQ community for reminding us all (queer and allies) that it gets better.

If you are experiencing bullying, reach out to a friend, a teacher, or a sibling and let them know what is happening. You don't (and shouldn't) go through it alone.

Most importantly, remember, tomorrow is a brand new day, and you can fill it with the most fun and crazy things.

You can also search 'bullying resources for kids' for immediate help. Although these resources will change over time, there are ALWAYS people who want to help a young person being bullied—all you have to do is reach out.

~

A LITTLE ABOUT ME, HEATHER KELLY, THE AUTHOR:

Yes, I've been bullied, and no, it didn't make me a better person. It just made me sad for a while.

I'm not a fan of people saying that every struggle makes you a better person. I don't see the use in that. Sometimes struggles make it harder to be the person you want to be.

The bullying made me feel like I wasn't worthy the way other people were worthy. I felt like I was on the outside of life and looking in; that I wasn't worthy of being in the center of life.

And that's not okay.

I didn't tell anyone at the time, but you know what? I would tell someone if I had to go through it again. I would want people like Sarah, Tim, and Casey on my side. Don't you?

And if you know someone going through it, you could be a Sarah or Tim or Casey for them.

When I showed this book to a publishing agent early on

in its creation, she said, well, wouldn't it be better if the bullying had some truth to it? Isn't that the best kind of story?

And I thought, no, that would be like blaming Kelly for being bullied.

It's also what bullying is all about—trying to make you feel like there's something wrong with you, when there isn't. Bullying tries to change your mind about who you are and what you deserve.

And you know what? Nobody can make you change your mind about yourself. Only you can decide what you think.

So I decided to publish this book myself, so I could make it what I wanted it to be, in all its silliness and fun.

And here it is—I hope you liked it.

And let me reiterate:

You are worthy. You can make a difference in this world and you belong here. In the center of things, being exactly who you are.

You might also have noticed that there are some references and quotes from sci-fi movies and books inside this book. They are Kelly and Tim's favorite fiction, and mine as well!

If you spot some of these references (in the gaming world these are called Easter eggs) write to me and let me know!

Maybe you can find them all!

Write to me through my website, www.heatherkellyau thor.com and let me know the things you spot in this book, tell me your story, or share with me what you hope to contribute to this world!

~

THE OFFICIAL(ish) BIO:

Heather Kelly explores the fabric of the universe by writing sci-fi, fantasy, and dystopian books for children and adults. She loves to hang out with her husband, three kids, and as many cats and bunnies as her family will allow. She loves playing One Night Ultimate Werewolf, Pokémon Go, and training for ridiculously long athletic adventures. Visit her websites for a longer bio: www.heatherkellyauthor.com.